Underwater

Helen Vivienne Fletcher

Copyright

For my same-name bestie, Helen.

Sad, poignant and darkly funny tales about Death.
Want it for free? Find out how at the end of the book.

One

MUM SAID I WASN'T taught to swim, I was just born knowing.

Tilly, on the other hand, never learnt, no matter how often we tried to teach her. She figured out how to not drown, though, and that seemed to be enough.

I don't think I've ever sat beside a body of water and not wanted to be a part of it. Not wanted to dive beneath the surface and feel the water encase me, like a fluid hug.

But that was before.

Now, I knew that no matter how long I sat beside the pool at Pine Hills Resort, I wouldn't get in.

The first thing I'd wanted to do, once I'd dumped my bag in my room and delivered Tilly to the kids' play area, was dive into the pool. But when I saw the number of people there, I chickened out. Instead I sat on the side, dangling my legs in the water and wishing they would all go away.

I swished my feet back and forth, making ripples across the surface. My skin tingled with the urge to dive in and swim. Stroke after stroke, until my arms would ache and my lungs would burn. Stroke after stroke until there would be no more thoughts, just ache and burn, ache and burn.

I rubbed sunscreen into my arms as I felt the sun sting at my skin. In a minute I'd get up and go find some shade. In a minute, but not just yet.

A couple of kids jumped in at the other end, sending water splashing up my legs. The tail of my sarong was wet, but instead of taking it off, I pulled it up higher. Again, I cursed the fact that the only swimsuit I owned now was a bikini. I missed the familiar grey one-piece from my swim-team uniform. Taking it off for the last time had been like removing a layer of skin.

Gran told me I looked fine – said all the things grandmas are supposed to say. I knew she just wanted to get me out the door. Not in a bad way, of course; she was doing a great job. She just didn't expect to be raising two kids in her retirement.

When we arrived here, the guy checking us in gave us the option of a family unit, or of me going in with the other teens and Tilly with the kids. Gran said it was up to me. The thought of being separated from her and Till made my stomach churn, but I could tell two weeks in the same cabin as Tilly and me wouldn't be much of a holiday for Gran. I told her it would be great for us to spend some time with kids our own age. So far I'd done everything I could to avoid talking to anyone my age, but Gran didn't need to know that.

A flash of red from the other side of the pool kept catching my eye. Red board shorts, reflecting on the surface of the pool. I couldn't help seeing it as blood, though, swirling and mixing with the water until everything was pink-tinged.

I looked up to force the thought out of my mind.

He was sitting on the other side of the pool, directly opposite me – the owner of the red board shorts. His eyes were closed, and he dangled his feet in the water.

It was strange. Everything seemed so fast here, so frenetic, but he was really still. I watched him, feeling some of the calm rub off on me.

He opened his eyes and frowned at me. I dropped my gaze, embarrassed I'd been caught staring. He was staring back, though, I could tell. I fiddled with the edge of my sarong, then forced myself to look up.

He met my eye. His frown deepened for a moment, then he smiled – one of those big, warm, goofy smiles that makes you want to smile back. I didn't, though. I looked down at the water and combed my fingers through my hair instead. He was still looking at me, I could tell. I hated the feeling of being watched, but I didn't want to meet his eye again.

"You're new here, aren't you?"

I jumped at the voice.

The girl was right behind me. She laughed. "Hey, sorry, didn't mean to startle you." She smiled. "I'm Clare."

"Bailey." I raised my hand to shade my eyes. The sun was right behind Clare, giving her a red and gold aura. The fact that her hair was incredibly blonde and shiny wasn't helping – I couldn't even tell what her face looked like. A flash of silver from her middle told me she had a belly button piercing. I'd been desperate to get mine done a few years ago, but Mum wouldn't let me. She told me I'd look back and regret it if I did. I think she was right. My ears weren't even pierced anymore; I'd let the holes grow over. The idea of metal impaling my skin just made me cringe.

"So, when did you get here?"

"Just this morning."

Her gaze drifted away from me. I didn't look, but I had a feeling she was watching the guy across the pool. Her eyes narrowed, then she turned back to me. She smiled. "Anyone show you around yet?"

I shook my head. That wasn't strictly true – the staff had shown us the basics when we checked in, but it was obvious Clare was trying to be nice and I didn't want to shut her down.

She reached out her hand to help me up. "Come on, I'll give you the tour."

I felt awkward taking her hand. But Gran kept telling me I needed to make more of an effort, so I smiled and let her help me up.

The tail of my sarong caught on my foot, and slipped from my waist as I stood.

Clare gasped. "Jeez, how'd you get that scar?"

"It's nothing." I grabbed the sarong, bundling it around my middle. "Nothing," I said again. "A-Append ..." I stuttered over the word, unable to get it out. My cheeks went hot and I stared at the ground.

Clare wrinkled her nose. "I had mine out and it doesn't look like that."

"Yeah ... well ..." I found I didn't have an answer for that.

The air stretched between us for a moment, then Clare gave a false laugh. "Remind me never to go to your surgeon."

I joined her in the forced laughter.

She gestured with her head. "Shall we go?"

She chattered as we walked. Apparently she was from one of a group of families who spent every summer at this resort. I couldn't imagine it – growing up with friends you saw once a year at the most. I knew myself well enough to see it would be too tempting to lie about the rest of your life. I'd been here half a day and I was doing it already.

"That's what I meant when I said you're new." She grinned, her teeth just as shiny as her hair. "It's your first year, isn't it?"

I nodded. "Yeah, my gran brought us."

"You staying in the family units?"

I shook my head. "Nah, I figured she needed a break from us."

Clare grinned. "Yeah, that's the attraction of this place. A holiday for the 'whole family'."

"Huh?"

Clare sighed. "They didn't give you the boy-girl lecture?"

I shook my head.

She pointed down a path. "Boys' cabins are down there. And the girls' cabins," she turned and pointed in the opposite direction, "are way over there." She grinned. "Peace of mind for the parents."

I frowned. "So what? We can drown and get eaten by bears as long as we don't go in the boys' cabins?"

Clare laughed. "Everything's fully supervised, life guards included, and the only bears you'll find around here are stuffed. Like I said – peace of mind."

My guess was that a lot went under the radar of the full supervision. If the kids here were anything like the ones at my old school, the cabins being separate wasn't going to stop much.

"Come on, I'll introduce you to some of the others."

I followed Clare down the hill into a shaded area. My head cleared as soon as we were out of the sun. I hadn't realised how much it had been hurting with the glare. Gran was probably right about me spending too much time indoors lately. I must have lowered my tolerance to natural light.

We rounded a corner and came out into an open grassy area. If I'd thought the pool was crowded, this place was packed. I recognised where we were now – the playground where I'd left Tilly was right next to us. I glanced over. Tilly was climbing up the ladder to the slide. I waved when she looked my way.

A girl sitting on one of the benches dropped something as Clare and I walked over to her.

Clare snorted. "You a smoker, Bailey? Apparently this is the place for it."

I shook my head. My coach back home wouldn't let me hang out with smokers. If he even thought he smelt smoke on my clothes, it meant a lecture on lung capacity, and extra drills.

"Shut up, Clare." The girl coughed, sending smoke everywhere. She stood and crushed her dropped cigarette underfoot. "You new here?" she said to me. Her hair was dark and cut short and spiky. It looked good, but I couldn't help thinking she looked like a kiwifruit.

"Yeah," I said.

She looked me up and down. It made me want to squirm, but I forced myself to hold her gaze. Finally she nodded. "I'm Amber. This is Jenny." She pointed to a girl sitting behind her.

"Hiya." Jenny's voice was bubbly and she beamed at me as she spoke.

Amber pointed across to a group of kids. "Eddie. Kristen. Tracey. Louise ..."

I tried to follow who she was pointing to. "I'm not going to remember any of those names, you know."

Amber shrugged. "Yeah, but now you can't blame me for it."

I glanced around. "So, all of you come here every year?"

Clare nodded. "Yep. Most of us since we were kids."

"Man, you must know all each other's secrets."

Jenny and Amber went quiet. Clare's face darkened for a moment, then she forced a smile. "You have no idea."

Sometimes there are those moments where you know you've said the wrong thing. I didn't know why, but this was one of them. "I didn't mean–"

"Bailey! Bailey, look at me!"

I let out a breath as Tilly interrupted me. I didn't know what I didn't mean, but I was glad to have an excuse to turn away.

Tilly was hanging upside down from the jungle gym. She let go to wave at me. "Look at me, Bailey!"

I had to swallow down the fear in my stomach. In my mind, I saw her crashing down on her head. I forced myself to grin. "Look at you, you little monkey," I called. I glanced back at Clare and the other girls. "See you later, yeah?"

Without waiting for an answer I walked over to the playground and stopped at the edge of the safety matting. "Be careful, Tilly," I called. She rolled her eyes at me. I shook my head. She might find being told to be careful annoying, but she was just lucky I wasn't marching over there and pulling her down from the bars. I'd have felt a hell of a lot better if I had, but I knew she'd never forgive me.

"You've got one too."

I jumped at the guy's voice.

He touched my arm. "Sorry, didn't mean to scare you."

"It's okay. Sorry," I mumbled. He left his hand on my arm for a second, then dropped it. It was the red-board-shorts guy from the pool. I knew that, but I pretended not to recognise him.

He gestured to Tilly. "A little adventurer." He smiled. "My brother's just the same." He pointed to a kid on the other side of the climbing frame. "That's Jack."

I opened my mouth, but couldn't think of anything to say. "Tilly likes climbing," I said eventually, and felt myself blush.

Now that I was closer to him, I could tell he hadn't really been frowning at me before. He just had one of those faces that always seem serious – kind of set, and harsh. Mum used to say that about me. She'd tell me off when we met new people. She said everyone thought I was sulking because I never smiled.

He glanced at me. "Haven't seen you around here before."

I shook my head. "First year."

He nodded. "I'm Adam." He grinned. "One of the regulars."

"I've heard about you lot." I attempted a smile, but he frowned.

"From Clare? She's–"

Tilly screamed. I spun round, running towards the play area before I even thought about it. Tilly was on the ground, her knee bloody. My stomach turned at the sight, and I felt dizzy. I sat down beside her. "Where does it hurt, Till?" I tried to make myself inspect her wound, but I couldn't.

Adam sat down next to me. "You're all right, aren't you? Just a little scrape." He grinned at Tilly, then turned back to the play area. "Jack, get down from there!"

Tilly shrunk away from him, crawling into my lap. The blood from her knee smeared across my sarong. I stared at it, then closed my eyes and pressed my hand against my mouth.

Adam raised his eyebrows. "I wouldn't have guessed you for a faints-at-the-sight-of-blood girl."

I opened my eyes. "I'm not. It's just–"

Tilly let out a howl. "I want to go home, Mummy."

I froze at the name. I didn't look at Adam, but I could feel his surprise without having to see it. Behind me I heard Clare giggle, then whispering from the other girls.

I picked Tilly up. "Come on, let's go get you a plaster." I didn't look back as I walked away.

Two

WHEN TILL WAS BORN, I used to tell people she was my baby.

One day, when she was three months old, I tried to take her to school with me. Mum thought she was asleep in her cot, and it was only when my backpack started crying that she realised. I don't know if I remember that, or just Mum telling us about it at every Christmas and birthday party.

Sometimes I try to remember what it was like being an only child, but I can't. It's like Till was always there, even in the moments I know happened before she was born.

"Hey, wait up."

I looked back. Adam was following us. I hesitated, then stopped and let him catch up. Tilly's legs were wrapped around my waist, and I could feel the blood seeping through my sarong, leaving a wet patch on my skin. I focused on his face to keep my head clear.

"You looking for the sick bay?"

I nodded. I'd actually been going to take Tilly back to Gran's room, but the sick bay was probably a better idea. The cut on her leg was still bleeding, and I had no idea whether she would need stitches or just a plaster.

"It's back this way. Come on, I'll show you." He smiled again, and this time I felt okay about smiling back.

"Thanks." I shifted Tilly as she slipped.

"Here, do you want me to take her?" He reached out to take Tilly from me, but I pulled away. Tilly squirmed and hid her face in my shoulder.

"No, she's fine."

He dropped his arms. "Sure."

I shifted Tilly again. She was getting too heavy for me to carry, really, but that didn't mean I was going to hand her off to a stranger. He scuffed his feet as he walked, kicking the gravel in front of him. I didn't want to be rude, but I couldn't think of anything to say.

He glanced up. "What's your name, by the way?"

I shook my head. "Bailey. Sorry."

"You're sorry your name is Bailey?" The corner of his lip twitched.

I laughed. "No, I just didn't realise I hadn't said."

"No worries."

We walked in silence for a couple of paces, then he grinned. "Though you should probably introduce your sister, as well."

"Sorry. This is Tilly." I smiled as I realised he'd referred to Tilly as my sister, not my daughter. That was going to be one less awkward conversation, at least. Hopefully Clare and the other girls had figured it out as well.

Tilly peeped out from my shoulder. Adam held out his hand to her, but she didn't take it.

"Nice to meet you, Tilly."

She stared at him, then smiled and hid her face again.

"Sorry, she's shy."

"Wow." Adam raised his eyebrows. "I've known you for, what ... five minutes? And you've already apologised like nine times."

I stared at him, unsure how to take that, then I shrugged. "Sorry?"

He nodded. "Good answer."

Adam waited while I took Tilly in to see the nurse. I wanted to tell him to go, but he was being so nice and that would have been rude. The nurse cleaned up Tilly's knee and gave her a Pooh Bear Band-Aid. Tilly scrunched up her nose and I could tell she was itching to tell the nurse she wasn't a baby.

The nurse gave us each a lollipop as we left. Tilly didn't seem to have any complaints about that.

"So, what's the damage?" Adam asked Tilly when we came out.

She showed him the plaster on her knee.

"Ah, Pooh Bear. I'm a fan of Tigger myself."

"Really?" Tilly stared at him.

"Of course."

Tilly grinned. "I like Piglet."

It was nearly lunchtime, and Adam offered to walk back to the dining room with us. I was glad, as I couldn't remember where it was and it hadn't been on Clare's tour. Actually, since it had been cut short, there hadn't been much on Clare's tour at all.

The dining room was more like a school lunch room – plastic trays and rows of tables. I half expected a food fight to break out.

Adam pulled us over to a self-service area. "You want to eat, you get food fast!" He dived straight into the food, as if to prove his point. "Trust me."

I laughed. "Whatever you say."

I loaded up a plate for me and Tilly, and we sat down. Adam was right about the need to get food quickly. The room was filling up fast, and the buffet was under siege, disappearing like everyone was preparing for the next ice age.

Tilly reached for the salt, but she knocked it over. The top came off and the salt spilt out over the table.

"Oh no! Salt avalanche!" I said.

Tilly stared at it, like she was going to cry.

"No use crying over spilt salt," Adam added. I couldn't help but smile.

Tilly reached forward and started drawing a pattern in it with her fingertip. I pushed her hand away. "Don't do that, Tilly." I picked up a pinch and threw it over my shoulder. After a second Tilly did the same.

I blushed as I realised Adam was watching us. "Our mum was superstitious," I said.

He shrugged. "It's not superstition if it works." He threw a pinch over his own shoulder, then scooped the rest of the salt back into the shaker.

Clare and the other girls were sitting at the table next to us. Clare had angled her chair away, keeping her back to us, but Jenny smiled at me and Amber gave me a nod. I gave a half wave in return.

I wasn't sure if I was imagining it, but it looked like Adam had shifted his chair too, inching it away from the other table. He didn't look up at them, at any rate.

One of the staff came in, herding a group of kids from the playground. She looked relieved when she saw me sitting with Tilly. I suppose I should have checked first, before taking Tilly off to the sick bay. Keeping track of that many kids would be enough to make the staff need the sick bay themselves.

Jack broke away from the group and rushed up to us. He tugged on Adam's sleeve, but then he stopped, staring at me and Tilly.

Adam sighed. "I'm sorry, you'll have to excuse Jack. He still thinks girls have cooties."

I looked at Tilly. "We haven't got cooties, have we Till?"

Tilly grinned and shook her head. "Girls don't have cooties," she said.

"Nope, it's boys who've got boy-germs, isn't it?"

Tilly nodded.

"Go on." Adam pushed Jack towards the buffet. "Get your lunch." He glanced over at Tilly and smiled. "You should show Tilly where the ice-cream is."

Amazingly, the prospect of ice-cream cut through the fear of both cooties and boy-germs. They ran off together, then sat down at the kids' table to eat.

I felt awkward alone with Adam. I wasn't used to talking to people I didn't know well, and it was like a bubble of silence had descended over our table. Adam didn't seem bothered by it, though; he was more focused on his food than anything else.

I took a breath. "You called Tilly my sister."

Adam stared at me. His frown deepened. "She is, isn't she?"

"Yeah, of course. I just mean ... How did you know she was my sister? After she called me Mummy?"

He shrugged. "I did the maths."

I frowned. "The maths?"

"I'm guessing you're about seventeen, and Tilly's got to be, what? Eight?" He gave a wry smile. "Even for a teen parent, that doesn't work."

I smiled. "Sixteen and seven, but your theory's right."

He nodded. "Does she do that often? Call you Mummy, I mean?"

I swallowed. "She ..." I glanced over at Tilly, not sure how much I should tell him. "Our parents died," I said eventually, "and Tilly ..." I shook my head. "I just feel mean correcting her, you know?"

The volume in the room rose as another group of kids arrived. I couldn't see any adults, other than the one or two staff members floating around.

Adam met my eye. I waited for him to change the subject, or make some stupid joke, just like everyone else did.

Instead he nodded. "My dad died when I was younger. Jack was only little." He shrugged. "I guess I kind of act like a dad to him too."

I felt something well up inside my chest. Most people didn't get it. If they didn't laugh, they either came out with pointless platitudes, or just stayed silent, not even bothering to hide their awkwardness. I ducked my head in an attempt not to cry.

"Are you okay?" Adam slid his hand across the table, but stopped just short of touching mine.

I nodded. "I'm fine, I just–"

A crash from the next table cut me off. I turned around. A girl was sprawled across the floor, her lunch tray beneath her.

"God, Frida, you're such a klutz." Clare laughed and kicked the apple from the girl's tray. "Can't you even walk in a straight line?"

"My name's Freya, not Frida," the girl said.

I got up and walked over. Adam stood too, but then he stopped, hovering just back from the table.

"Are you okay?" I asked Freya.

She nodded. "Yeah, I just ..." She patted at the ground in front of her. "I knocked my contact out."

Clare made a noise in her throat. "Just go back to wearing glasses, if you can't cope with them."

As far as I could see, Freya had tripped over Clare's bag which had been left in the aisle beside her table. I pushed it under Clare's chair.

"Could happen to anyone," I said to Freya.

Clare rolled her eyes. I frowned at her. She'd seemed nice earlier, but now she was acting like a total cow.

Freya grabbed at something I couldn't see, then lifted up the contact lens. "Got it."

Clare scrunched up her face. "Don't put it back in while we're eating. It's gross." She stabbed at her salad.

That much salad dressing is gross, I nearly said. Instead I turned back to Freya. "Here, let me get that." I reached down to pick up her tray.

Clare scoffed. "Of course, you're used to picking up after messy kids, aren't you, Bailey?" She smirked. "Being a teen-mum and all."

Clare had picked her moment perfectly. The room was quiet with everyone focused on Freya's accident. A couple of girls at another table giggled, and I could hear whispers starting already.

Amber frowned and Jenny said something under her breath. She met my eye for a second, then looked away. Apparently my supposed parenthood had turned me into a total pariah.

I straightened up and stared at Clare. She stared back, raising her eyebrows into a challenge. I wanted to tell her I wasn't

Tilly's mum, but even if I had been, that was no reason to act like such a bitch. My throat hurt as I tried to form the words into a sentence.

Adam stepped forward and took Freya's tray from me. "Come on, Clare, you're not that thick."

Clare's cheeks went pink and she forced her mouth into a tight smile. "Really, Adam? Name calling?"

He stared at her, then raised his voice so the whole room could hear. "Tilly's Bailey's sister, not her daughter." He turned back to Clare. "Just in case any of the rest of you are as mathematically challenged as Clare."

Clare's cheeks turned from pink to red. I felt mine do the same.

I turned back to Freya. "Are you okay now?"

She nodded. "Yeah, I'm–"

I didn't wait for her to finish. I walked past her and Adam, and through the door to outside.

The temperature had dropped, the air cool against my burning cheeks. I pressed my hands against them.

"Hey, Bailey?" Freya had followed me out.

I composed my face, then turned towards her.

She came forward, hesitantly. "Thanks, you didn't have to do that."

"It was nothing."

"Believe me, it was something."

I glanced at Freya. I wanted to ask her what she meant. Was Clare really that horrible? Freya tipped her head back and touched her eye, fitting the lens back into place.

"Freya–" I stopped as the door to the dining hall slammed.

"Here we go." Freya rolled her eyes. Clare had followed us outside.

"Freya, wait up," she called.

Freya didn't look up, but waited for Clare to catch up to us.

"I'm sorry. I was being a cow." Clare smiled and shrugged at the same time. "Forgive me?"

Freya shook her head. "It's fine." She still didn't look at Clare, though. Out of the corner of my eye, I saw Adam emerge from the dining room. He paused in the doorway, watching us.

Clare turned to me. "You too, Bailey. I'm sorry. Clearly I got the wrong end of the stick." She tried the smile-shrug thing again.

I frowned. "And if I *was* Tilly's mum?"

"But you're not, right?"

"No, but ..." *What business is it of yours?* I wanted to say. More than that, I wanted to tell her to get stuffed. I felt Freya glance up at me.

Clare's eyes narrowed, then she shrugged. "Well, sorry, anyway." She hesitated, then walked away.

I hadn't meant to, but I'd rattled Clare. She must be used to everyone accepting her fake apologies, but that's what she was: fake-nice.

Adam was still hovering. He followed Clare with his eyes, then looked back at me. I turned away. The tension between those two was intense. Whatever their history, I didn't want to get involved.

I looked back at Freya. "Will you show me the way back to the cabins?"

Earlier I'd dumped my bag in the cabin the guy had shown me to, but I hadn't really had time to check it out. Freya told me it was two girls to each, random assignment.

"Just pray you don't end up with Clare." Freya giggled and I forced a laugh. I had enough trouble sleeping as it was. If I ended up with Clare, I'd be high-tailing it back to the family units.

Amber greeted us on the deck outside my cabin. "Switch with me?"

"Huh?"

She handed me the bag I'd left on my bed. "Switch with me. I'm in with Freya, and Jenny's supposed to be in with you. Jenny and I are always in the same cabin." She hurried through the explanation, then looked from me to Freya. I glanced at Freya and she shrugged.

"Fine with me," I said.

"Cool, thanks." She handed me my bag, and darted off into the other cabin with Jenny. We heard them laughing inside.

Freya shook her head. "They did that last year too. They're inseparable."

I spent most of the afternoon lying on my bed, reading my book. Freya asked if I wanted to come back to the pool with her, but I went up to the kids' area to check on Tilly instead. The kids were all inside, working on a craft, and Tilly was happily chatting to Jack, so I slipped away before she saw me.

The whole time, I was itching to get in the pool. I waited until the sky outside had turned from blue, to indigo, to charcoal, then told Freya I was going for a walk.

"Remember curfew's at ten," she called after me.

I nodded and waved to show I'd heard her. Really, I didn't think it would matter. Since I'd arrived that morning, I'd only seen a couple of staff members. Despite Clare's insistence that everything was fully supervised, neither of them had seemed that bothered as to what I was doing.

I followed the path down to the pool. The gate was locked, the sign on it clearly saying no swimming after eight p.m. I checked the time – quarter past nine. My guess would be the closure was due to not wanting to pay night-lifeguards. That was fine; I wasn't planning on getting into strife.

I scaled the fence and dropped down on the other side.

It felt good to be able to strip down to my swimsuit and not have to worry about anyone looking at me. In the fading light, the scar was just a dark line – passable as a birthmark.

I stretched my arms above my head, then dived. The swoosh as my body broke the surface disorientated me for a second, and then I was off. I swam three lengths before surfacing. My breath forced itself into gasps, only partly from the exertion. I dipped my head under the water as the tears started.

I swam another length, slower this time. I let my body stretch and glide in the water, easing the kinks from the long car journey.

Above me the stars appeared. I floated on my back, watching them.

"*Twinkle, twinkle, little star ...*" My voice echoed in my water-filled ears. I closed my eyes and let myself drift.

Mum used to hate it when I did that. She said she was scared I'd fall asleep and slowly sink to the bottom where I'd drown. Dad told her not to worry. He thought if I fell asleep, the water would wake me. Part of me wanted to see what would happen if I did slip beneath the surface in my sleep. I dreamed of waking underneath the water, growing a mermaid's tail.

A bird let out a warning cry, breaking the stillness of the night. I twisted upright as it beat through the air above my head.

"Hello?"

The birds all around were shifting, calling to each other. I scanned the bushes, looking for what had startled them. A dark shape caught my eye.

"Hello?" I called again, my voice betraying the fear in my stomach.

"Bailey?" Tilly called from behind me.

I turned towards her voice. She was on the path, walking towards me. I looked back to where I'd seen the figure in the bushes. It was gone.

"Tilly, come here. Quickly." I pulled myself out of the pool.

"The gate's locked." Tilly fiddled with the latch, trying to open it.

"Don't worry about it. Here." I chucked my clothes over the fence, then climbed over. "Are you okay?" I wrapped Tilly in a hug.

She squirmed away from me. "You're all wet! Why didn't you bring a towel?"

I shook my head. My heart was throwing itself at the inside of my rib cage.

Tilly stared at me through the dark. "Bailey?" Her voice cracked with the fear she was drawing from me.

I forced myself to calm down. "It's okay. You just startled me, that's all." I looked down at her. "What are you doing out here? Why aren't you in bed?"

She stared at the ground. I watched her trace a pattern in the dirt with her toe.

"Tilly?"

She looked up at me. "I don't want to stay by myself."

"Tilly–"

"Please? I want to sleep in your room."

I rubbed my face and sighed. Truth was, I'd feel so much safer knowing Tilly was where I could keep an eye on her, but what was that teaching her? She already knew the world wasn't a safe place; she didn't need my fears compounding hers.

"Okay," I said. "But just for tonight."

Tilly grinned. "Thanks, Bailey."

I pulled my clothes on over my wet swimsuit, then took her hand as we walked back to my cabin.

"Why were you swimming in the dark?"

I glanced down at Tilly. "It's less busy."

"But the fence was locked."

"Yeah. I climbed over."

She frowned at her feet. "That's breaking and entering."

I stopped. "Tilly ..."

She looked up at me, waiting for me to answer. I stared at her. "It's not the same," I said, finally. It wasn't much of an answer and I knew it.

She regarded me, searching my face, then finally shrugged. "If you say so."

I let out a breath.

Freya was in the bathroom when we got back to the cabin. I changed into my pyjamas and towel dried my hair, then waited outside the bathroom door for her.

"Oh, hey." She grinned as she saw me. "I was just about to send out a search party."

I gave a weak smile in return. "Yeah, well ..." I stepped in her way as she went to open the door to our room. "Listen, my little sister–"

"The one Clare thought was your daughter?" Freya grinned.

"Yeah, Tilly." I sighed. "She doesn't sleep so well, so I was wondering if it would be okay if–"

"If she slept in here? Yeah sure."

"It would just be for tonight."

Freya made a dismissive motion with her hand. "Don't worry about it. She can stay as long as you need."

I smiled. "Don't tell her that, she'll never leave."

Freya raised her eyebrows. "Is that a smile, Bailey? That's got to be a first."

I frowned. Everyone was always telling me I was too serious, but I didn't think I was. Half the time I felt like they just didn't get my sense of humour.

Freya laughed. "I'm kidding. Don't worry about it."

I hesitated in the doorway to our room. Tilly was sitting on my bed. She'd taken down the picture of Mum and Dad I'd pinned on the wall, and was sitting there, staring at it.

"You must be Tilly."

Tilly shoved the photo under the pillow as Freya came into the room. I caught Freya's eye, but she didn't say anything.

"Did you do these pictures?" Freya pointed to Tilly's drawings, which I'd pinned up next to the photo.

Tilly nodded.

"Tilly's quite the artist with a felt pen," I said.

Freya leaned over the bed to look at them, making Tilly shrink back. "Pretty cool, kid. Much better than I could do, anyway."

I felt a swell of pride at that. Most kids Tilly's age were still drawing stick figures, but Tilly had spent the last few months drawing abstract patterns with swirls and lines. "Tilly's going to be an artist someday, aren't you bub?"

Tilly shook her head. She pulled the pictures off the wall and put them face down on the floor.

I glanced at Freya and shrugged. "She's shy," I said.

I climbed into the bed next to Tilly and changed the subject. "You want a story?"

"Yeah, if you're offering." Freya grinned at me.

I rolled my eyes. "Tilly?"

She nodded.

I told her Cinderella from memory. The version with the cut-off toes and the eyes getting pecked out. Mum and Dad never let us read that version, because they thought it would give us nightmares. That didn't seem to matter anymore.

Tilly and Freya both fell asleep before I'd finished. Tilly's head rolled against my shoulder, and her lips parted as she relaxed. Freya's breath deepened into something that wasn't quite a snore.

"Night, Tilly," I said to her as I turned out the light. "Night, Mum and Dad," I said to the photo under my pillow.

* * * *

THE NIGHT MY PARENTS died, it was a car outside that woke me. That seems ridiculous now, given everything else that happened that night. All the noise that must have been going on and yet it took the headlights of a car reversing into the driveway across the street to wake me up.

I remember I lay there for a good ten minutes before realising anything was wrong; before I noticed Tilly wasn't in her bed.

The thing I can't remember, though, is what I thought about in that time. It seems like it should have been something important, something I should be able to recall. But I don't remember anything.

I think I was actually falling asleep again when I heard the crash downstairs. I jerked upright, and that's when I saw Tilly's bed was empty.

"Tilly?"

She didn't answer. She knew enough to stay hidden, even if I hadn't figured out what was going on. I went looking for her, thinking she must have been sleep walking. She'd done it a few times before, mostly when she was little. It was a big part of the reason we slept in the same room – so I could go find her without having to wake Mum and Dad.

The TV was on downstairs, though the lights were off. I could see Mum's silhouette slumped on the sofa, lit by an infomercial for window cleaner.

I remember laughing, thinking of all her lectures about getting a proper night's sleep and not dozing off in front of the TV. I thought of going in there and covering her up with a blanket. She was such a light sleeper, though, and so grumpy when woken up suddenly. So I left her there, didn't even go in the room.

I didn't turn the lights on. I'm glad of that now, because even though I never saw them, the images give me nightmares.

Three

APPARENTLY I DIDN'T have nightmares as a baby – I was never scared of the dark. I thought it was strange how Mum told me that. How would she know what I dreamt about?

She said she'd often come into my room at night and I'd be awake, just staring into the dark like I could see something there that she couldn't.

I don't remember the last time I slept through the night without at least one dream that left me clenching my fists and trying to slow my breathing as I woke.

• • • •

I FELT SICK AS I WOKE up on my third day at Pine Hills. In the time between being fully asleep and fully awake, I'd been dreaming that an Alsatian dog had climbed into the bed with me. The heat from its body left me drenched in sweat, but I was too sleepy to push it away.

As I woke properly, I realised there was no dog, but Tilly was curled up against my stomach. For a moment I thought she'd wet the bed, but it was just sweat from the two of us sharing body heat all night.

I groaned, and retrieved my arm from underneath her. "Till, you've got to start sleeping in your own cabin."

Tilly's eye's flickered, but she didn't open them. She'd been employing that tactic a lot lately. Rather than argue with me, she'd pretend not to hear.

I left her lying in the bed, and went off to the bathroom.

I hesitated outside the door as I heard one of the toilets flush, then it opened and Jenny stumbled out. Her hair was puffed out around her, a cross between a bird's nest and a halo. She gave me a sleepy smile and went back to her room.

Clare had invited people to her cabin last night. Amber had asked me if I wanted to join them, but I'd said no. I'd avoided Clare since the first day, and I was pretty sure she was trying to do the same. Fortunately she was in a cabin a couple of blocks over, which made it easier for both of us.

I think Freya was annoyed with me for turning down the invitation. They didn't ask her, and I think she'd wanted to tag along with me.

I'd been trying to get up early in the mornings so I didn't run into other girls in the bathroom. It didn't always work. With one bathroom to three cabins, and two girls in each – or three in our case, with Tilly insisting on sleeping in my bed – it was hard to find a time when there was no-one else there.

I pinned my fringe back so I could wash my face. My old face peered back at me from the mirror. Fifteen years without a fringe, and now my face looked naked without it. I ran my finger over one of the scars on my forehead. They weren't so bad now, just silvery-yellow lines. Nothing like the one on my stomach. The colour reminded me of maggots, though, and it made my stomach turn.

I shivered, and washed my face as quickly as I could, then shook my hair back out over my shoulders. I combed my fringe, making it sit flat over my forehead. It crackled, dry from a lifetime of chlorine. But the dark colour was bleached with highlights from the sun, now, making it less harsh.

I looked up and caught Clare's reflection in the mirror.

She met my eye and shrugged. "All the showers in our bath-room are taken." She held up her towel. "You don't mind, do you?"

I shook my head. "Go for it."

She held my eye for a second, but didn't say anything. She was right by the door; she could only just have stepped in the room. But I could tell she'd seen the scars.

If she asked, I could lie again. I could tell her about some other fake surgery or childhood accident. She hadn't believed me about the appendix, though, and she was smart enough to put two and two together.

She smiled. "You should wear your hair out like that. It's really pretty."

I let out a breath. Clare was hard to figure out, but I was fairly sure that was her way of letting me know she wouldn't say anything.

Freya and Tilly were up when I got back to the cabin. They were sitting on my bed, and Freya was teaching Tilly a clapping game.

She looked up as I came in. "I see we had a midnight visitor again?"

I smiled. "Yeah, Tilly arrived after you went to sleep."

"Bit of a worry the staff haven't noticed she's not sleeping in her cabin."

I laughed. "I know. Fully supervised is a joke."

The truth was, the whole thing seemed a bit of a con. As far as I could tell, the staff didn't supervise anything. The whole attraction of this place was supposed to be that the parents could dump the kids into someone else's care and have a holiday themselves. From what I could see, everyone under the age of twenty-five was running wild.

I slid my hand under my pillow – my photo wasn't there. I checked down the back of the bed but I couldn't see it there either. Tilly avoided my eye, and I could tell she'd put it somewhere. I watched her, but I didn't ask.

"There's a party down at the pool today."

I glanced up at Freya.

"You wanna go?" She frowned as she voiced the question. I could tell she knew I was going to say no. I'd said no to everything so far. There was no obligation to take part in any of the organised events. I think the staff probably wanted us to – easier to keep an eye on us and all that – but they didn't enforce it. Freya seemed gung-ho about going to everything, but I wondered if it was just an attempt to fit in. Unlike the other girls, who were all permanently split into little groups, she didn't seem to have any close friends here. She said she'd only been coming to Pine Hills a couple of years, so was still considered a newbie, like me. I think she was hoping we'd be the core of a new group.

I shook my head. "I was going to head up to see Gran. I might stop by later, though?" I added at her disappointed look.

Freya's face brightened. "Cool, I might see you down there then."

I dropped Tilly off at the kids' area then headed up the hill to Gran's cabin.

Dad always used to call Gran a gin-and-tonic parent. I'd never really understood what he meant – as far as I could see she was a great mother to Mum, and about as far from an alcoholic as you could get. When Tilly and I moved in with her, though, I think I saw what he meant. She'd greeted us at the door with a gin and tonic in hand, and I didn't know whether to laugh or cry. But it was a prop, really – it went with the flowing scarves and perfume.

The adults' cabins were a lot swisher than the ones we were staying in. Each had its own bathroom, kitchenette and separate bedroom. No wonder there weren't many adults eating in the dining hall. If you could make your own food, and avoid hanging out with a hundred teens and kids, why would you eat in there?

Through the window I could see Gran reclining on the couch. She got up to let me in when I knocked.

"Bailey." She frowned at me, then ushered me inside.

She poured me a glass of orange juice, then sat me down on the couch. "Tell me everything, darling. Have you made any new friends?"

Edith Piaf's *Je Regrette Rien* blared from the stereo, and Gran got up to turn it down.

"Yeah, I've made a few friends," I said while her back was turned.

"Mmm ... that's good," she said. It was the same "mmm" Mum used to use when she didn't believe me.

"My roommate, Freya," I said, "she's really lovely. And there's this guy, Adam–"

"A boy! That's exciting."

I shook my head. "Not like that. I haven't talked to him since the first day." I bit my lip. I hadn't meant to tell her that. She'd been worried I'd avoid talking to anyone here, and that's exactly what I'd been doing.

Gran sighed. I could see she was concerned about me, but I didn't know what to tell her. It wasn't that I was scared; I just didn't want to talk to people. I didn't want new people in my life. It wasn't worth it.

I waited for her lecture to start. *You can't avoid people forever, Bailey.* She stared at me, the lines in her face ageing her to the grandmother she pretended not to be.

"I'm okay, Gran. I promise."

She smiled at me. "You're more like your mother than you realise, Bailey."

I stared at her. My mum was beautiful and strong, and probably never avoided anything in her life. I frowned. "But–"

I was cut off by a knock on the door. Gran glanced at it, then back at me. "Trust me, you are, love." She walked over and opened the door.

"Hey, I was looking for Bailey?"

I looked up as I heard Adam's voice. "Hey?" I was embarrassed by the wobble in my voice turning that into a question. I got up to cover it.

Gran smiled. "Come in, young man." She turned and winked at me. "I'm just going to freshen my drink."

I blushed as Gran wafted her way over to the kitchen.

"Come in," I said to Adam. I went to sit back down, then stood up again and moved over to the door instead. "How did you know I was here?" I leant against the door in a horribly awkward attempt to look casual. My face was so hot; I must have been turning purple.

Adam didn't seem to notice. "Freya told me you'd gone to see your Gran." He raised his eyebrows. "She said you weren't coming to the pool party, so I thought I'd try to convince you." He gave a little smile, taking the edge off his frown.

I hesitated. I'd been avoiding him since we talked on the first day. Apart from Freya, he was the only person I'd properly got along with since I arrived. I wasn't really looking to make friends, though.

"I was going to hang out with Gran today," I said.

"Don't be silly, sweetie," Gran called from the kitchen. She popped her head around the corner. "You don't want to spend all day with the old fogeys. Go have fun."

Now I had no excuse not to go. My only option was to be excruciatingly rude, and tell him I didn't want to go. If I did that, I wouldn't be able to lie to Gran anymore about how well things were going with my new friends. I forced a smile for Gran's benefit, then turned back to Adam. "Sounds like we're going to the pool."

I didn't talk to Adam as we walked. He didn't seem like much of a talker, but I think even he could tell how awkward this was. He looked at me a couple of times, but I pretended not to notice. Out of the corner of my eye I could see his frown growing deeper.

We stopped by the playground to check on Tilly and Jack. It was strange, because we didn't discuss doing that – we just both walked there automatically. I smiled. In a weird way, it was nice to be in sync with someone.

Tilly was on top of the jungle gym again, Jack beside her. My stomach tensed, but I didn't call out.

"Jack's holding her hand." Adam glanced at me, then pointed. "Guess he got over his fear of cooties."

I frowned as I watched them. Jack was holding on to her to help her balance, stopping her from falling.

"How old were you, when your dad died?"

"Huh?" Adam looked up at me.

I cursed myself for being so blunt. After my long silence I couldn't blame him for being surprised at what I'd come out with. "Sorry." I shook my head. "It's just, you said ... It doesn't matter."

Adam shrugged. "It's okay. I was ten. Jack was just about to turn two."

I chewed on the inside of my cheek. "Did you talk about him after he died?"

"Yeah, of course. Why?"

I watched Tilly laughing as she tipped upside down. "Tilly won't talk about Mum and Dad. Not ever. She doesn't even like looking at photos." I didn't look up at Adam. I could feel him watching me, though.

He touched my arm. "Bailey–"

I pulled away from him. "We should get down to the pool."

Adam was in the water as soon as we got there. He tried to get me to come in, but I sat down on a sun lounger next to Freya instead.

She grinned. "Did Adam drag you down here?"

I shrugged. "I said I'd be down later, didn't I?"

Clare ignored me, but Amber and Jenny chatted to Freya and me. They were sharing a sun lounger, Jenny perched on the end of it leaning against Ambers legs. It wasn't really big enough for two people and it tipped every time one of them got excited or gestured too wildly – something they did frequently, as it turned out.

Adam and the other guys splashed about, trying to get our attention. Freya flashed them a smile, then eventually jumped in the pool too, but the rest of us ignored them. It's weird how that happens – guys trying to impress girls by acting like idiots. I guess they don't realise the things that impress girls aren't the same as the silly things other boys are impressed by.

Clare rubbed at her shoulders. "Ugh, I'm peeling."

"Here." I passed her the sunscreen from my bag. She raised her eyebrows but didn't take the tube.

"Thanks, but I'd rather find some shade."

I wasn't quite sure how to take that. From her tone, she was trying to insult me by not taking the sunscreen, but what kind of insult is getting yourself sunburnt? I hesitated, then put it back in my bag. "Sure."

Clare made a noise in her throat, and got up and walked away. Jenny leant over to me as she did. "Hey, don't take it personally, eh?"

I looked up at her. "Huh?"

"Clare." Jenny combed her fingers through her hair, making it spring out around her. "It's not about you, really. She and Adam. They used to date."

Amber sighed. "Really, Jenny? Are we going to air all our dirty laundry in public?" She leaned back on the sun lounger and shaded her eyes with her elbow.

Jenny clicked her tongue. "It's not like it's a secret."

"True, true."

I shook my head. "It's okay. They're so weird around each other, I'd figured as much."

Amber raised her head and peered at me from under her hand. "See, what you've got to understand, Bailey, is some of these families have been coming here for years." She made a sweeping gesture, encompassing the whole pool area. "Most of us, three or four years. Six at the max. Clare and Adam's families, however ..."

I smiled. "So what? They're like royalty here?"

Amber scoffed and Jenny cracked up.

"Royalty? No. More like dysfunctional grandparents at a family reunion." Jenny giggled. She sat up and pointed across the pool to where Clare was opening the gate. "Clare started coming here when she was six. Adam," she pointed to his figure diving under the water, "two years later when they were both eight. You know the story. Boy meets girl, girl has a temper tantrum over boy hogging the swings ..." Jenny grinned. "Naturally they hated each other until they both hit thirteen and puberty set in."

I frowned. This was the most I'd even heard Jenny talk. I felt bad because I'd written her off as ditzy – Amber's side-kick. Jenny was bubbly, but that didn't make her stupid. To think of her as ditzy had been totally unfair of me.

"End of last summer, they split," Amber cut in. "As far as we can tell, they didn't speak all year."

I shook my head. "So what does all that have to do with me?"

Amber raised her eyebrows and regarded me.

Jenny giggled. "Are you kidding? You haven't noticed?"

I shrugged. "What? Just because Adam and I talked a couple of times?" I shook my head again. "I'm not interested in him."

They both stared at me.

"What? I'm not."

Amber smirked. "The lady doth protest too much, me-thinks."

I frowned. I could feel my face settling into a scowl. "It doesn't matter anyway," I said. "They're obviously still into each other."

"That's for sure."

Amber flicked a mosquito off Jenny's arm, gently rubbing the spot where it had bitten her. "Ugh, you're burning up out here." She stood and pulled off her T-shirt. Jenny followed suit.

"You coming?" Amber nodded towards the pool.

I shook my head.

"Come on, you'll bake if you stay here." Jenny stripped off her shorts and joined Amber at the side of the pool.

"Nah," I shook my head. "I can't swim." I cursed myself for the idiocy of that lie. I was bound to be found out, and it left the door open for offers of swimming lessons.

Amber wrinkled her nose. "That sucks." She shrugged. "Come on, Jenny."

I watched them splash around for a while. Amber was pretty strong in the water. With the right trainer, she could probably compete.

Jenny spent most of her time splashing and flirting with the guys. I tried to remember what that was like – when getting in the water was just a time to muck around and play. For most of my life, the pool had been a serious time – training, getting fit, working.

I stood up.

"Where're you going?" Freya called to me. Adam and Jenny glanced around too.

"Going to find some shade," I called back. "See you later though." I glanced back when I got to the gate. The girls had gone back to swimming, but Adam was watching me leave. I waved at him, then turned away.

· · · ·

THAT EVENING, THERE was a campfire out in the bush. I hadn't been planning to go, but Freya had pulled out a rather extreme sad look so I'd given in.

The kids ran around in the early evening, chasing each other with sparklers. Tilly wouldn't join them until I got up too. I pulled my hair back into a bun to avoid singeing it, then lit two sparklers – one for me and one for Tilly.

"Try writing your name," I said.

Tilly stared, fascinated by the letters trailing after my sparkler. Her own sparkler burned, forgotten, in her hand.

I got as far as B-A-I-L before it went out. I lit another, spelling out "Tilly" this time. Tilly giggled as it burned out halfway through the Y.

"Lucky I call you 'Till', isn't it?"

"Shorter names are definitely better for sparklers." Adam came up beside me, and took one out of the packet. He lit it with a cigarette lighter from his pocket, then caught my eye. "I don't smoke," he said. He raised the lighter, and it flashed silver, lit by the sparkler. "It was Dad's." He slipped it back in his pocket.

I pressed my lips together. I hadn't realised my disapproval was so obvious. He raised the sparkler, spelling out "Adam" before it burned out.

"Jack's not so keen on spelling." Adam pointed over to where Jack was running in and out of the trees, his sparkler held above him like a beacon. I glanced down at Tilly. She didn't seem at all keen on running around, though I wished she would. She was shivering, her arms clasped tightly around herself.

"Are you cold, Tilly?"

She shook her head, determined not to admit it. I sighed, then caught Adam's eye again and laughed. "Is Jack this stubborn?" I asked him.

"Worse."

I turned back to Tilly. "Come on, bub." I pulled her over to the fire. "Let's get you warmed up."

I borrowed a blanket from Amber and wrapped it around the two of us. She stopped shivering, but I could hear her teeth chattering against each other.

"You want a marshmallow?" I asked her.

Tilly nodded. I stuck one on a stick for her, but then she was too scared to hold it close enough to the fire.

Adam took it from me. "Jack's exactly the same. Loves sparklers but is terrified of the actual fire."

I smiled. I don't think Tilly was really all that scared, she was just tired. My guess was neither of us was sleeping well, as we half woke every time the other moved.

Adam handed her the marshmallow when it was done.

"What do you say, Tilly?"

She gave Adam a shy smile. "Thank you."

Adam grinned. "You're welcome, Tilly." He wrapped himself in a blanket and sat down next to me. "Much better manners than Jack."

Jack had given up on running around with his sparkler, and was sitting on the other side of the campfire scoffing marshmallows straight from the bag.

Adam laughed as he caught sight of him. "God, I'd hate to be on duty in the kids' cabins tonight."

As if on cue, a lady in a bright pink T-shirt started rounding up the kids. I wondered if I should go back with Tilly, since she would most likely be heading up to my cabin at some point anyway. But the lady took her hand, and Tilly glanced back at me.

"You okay?" I mouthed.

She nodded and rubbed at her eyes. Maybe it would be better if I left her. If she was this tired, she might actually fall asleep and stay in her own bed for once.

She looked really tiny next to the woman, only coming up to her hip. She'd used to look like that standing between Mum and Dad, when she'd swing on their hands. Same as I did once, I guess. I watched until they turned the corner and went out of sight.

With the kids gone, the atmosphere was much calmer, everyone relaxing around the fire in a sleepy sort of way.

Someone had picked up a guitar and was making an attempt at tuning it. I caught sight of Clare, arriving late. She caught my eye and stared at me. Her expression was neutral, but it felt like she was trying to stare me out. I looked away, not caring if it seemed like I was the first to back down. When I looked back, she was heading off to sit down.

I shivered, and rearranged the blanket around myself as I felt the chill creep in where Tilly had been sitting.

"You cold?" Adam lifted the edge of his blanket, wrapping it around my shoulder.

I pulled away. "No, I'm fine."

"And Tilly's the stubborn one?" Adam laughed. He took my hand, rubbing it between his. "Your hands are freezing."

"So are yours." I laughed. "I guess we're all stubborn."

He pressed the back of his hand to his cheek and chuckled. "I'll get us some hot chocolate. That'll warm us up." He headed over to where people were lining up to pour mugfuls out of a big urn. I shivered again as he did. Much as I pretended I was fine by myself, it was a lot warmer sitting close to someone else.

Adam handed me a mug then sat down, wrapping the blanket around us again. I felt awkward as I realised his arm was around me too, but it was obvious this was the normal thing. Everywhere I looked, people were paired up under blankets, huddling to keep warm. Jenny and Amber were tucked up together, eating roasted marshmallows from sticks, and Freya was wrapped up with a guy I thought might be Eddie. They looked ridiculous – he was a lot taller than her, so the blanket made a cave over her head. His face was in shadows, but the light from the fire glinted off his glasses, making two cat-like eyes.

Freya waved as she saw me looking, and I raised my mug in greeting back.

"It gets pretty cold here at night," Adam said.

I nodded. "I hadn't noticed it so much inside."

I sipped at the chocolate and felt it warm my stomach. Then I shivered again, in that weird way you do when you start to warm up.

Adam laughed. "You still going to say you're not cold?"

I shrugged. "Stubborn I'll admit to. But cold ...?"

"It's all right. Me too."

I glanced around the fire. Three days here, and I still only knew the names of about half the people, and most of those were the ones I'd met on the first day. True to my word, I couldn't remember any of the people Amber had pointed out to me. I guess it didn't really matter. When we left here in a couple of weeks, I'd probably never see any of them again. Unless Gran decided to make us "regulars".

"So, where are you from?" I asked Adam. "I forget people come from all over the place to stay here."

He grinned. "Yeah, it's a mixed bag for sure. I'm from Auckland. You?"

I swallowed my mouthful of hot chocolate. "Wellington originally, though Gran's in Paihia, so we moved up there a couple of months ago."

"Jenny lives in the Bay of Islands. You should catch up with her when you go back."

I nodded. That might actually be good. I hadn't started school in Paihia yet, so it might be kind of nice to know at least one person. The police had thought it would be safer for us to move away from Wellington, rather than have Gran come down to live with us. I agreed – being in another city did make me feel more secure – but leaving my home was just another thing I'd lost.

"So have you been out surfing yet?"

I shook my head. "Don't know how. My dad was a surfer, though. Mum too … kind of." I never actually saw Mum get out on a board, but she always swore she was brilliant. She'd wanted to teach me someday.

Adam nodded. "My dad taught me when I was Jack's age."

"Does Jack surf too?"

Adam shook his head. "He's keen though." Adam frowned, and for a moment it was like I could hear his thoughts. All the things his dad wouldn't be able to teach Jack. Just like all the things I'd have to teach Tilly because Mum and Dad weren't going to be there to do it.

Adam grinned. "Perhaps you and Tilly could come out with us. I'll teach you all in one go."

I laughed. "Judging by Tilly's adventures on the jungle gym, I'm not sure either of us have the balance for it."

"Yeah, you've–" Adam stopped suddenly and groaned. He smacked his hand against his forehead. "Sorry, I'm being an idiot. I forgot you can't swim."

I opened my mouth to contradict him, then stopped myself. "Yeah," I said. I stared at the fire, then looked away as my eyes blurred.

Adam shifted beside me. He seemed to be waiting for me to continue, but there wasn't much I could say. Even if it had been true, I'm not sure there would have been much more to tell. Again I cursed myself for telling such a stupid lie.

"Jenny said that's why you didn't come in the pool. I felt like a dick for dragging you down there this morning."

I shook my head. "Nah, it's fine."

Adam shifted again, then he grinned. "Perhaps I could teach you to swim, too?"

I laughed. "Learn to swim at a surf beach? That sounds like a disaster waiting to happen." I shook my head again. "It's fine, really. It was actually kind of nice today hanging out with Jenny and Amber."

Adam nodded. "Yeah, they're cool. Amber's in Auckland too, so we hang out sometimes."

The guitar was tuned now, and someone was playing it – soft chords making a sleepy soundtrack. I yawned and rubbed at my eyes. I wondered if it would be weird if I asked him about Clare. Probably, since I didn't really know either of them that well. Curiosity was scratching at my stomach, though, making me want to know the other side of the story.

"So, do you get out surfing much?" I asked instead.

He nodded. "Not as much as I'd like, though."

I smiled. "Damn schoolwork getting in the way?"

"Schoolwork. Part-time job."

"Where do you work?" I glanced up at him.

He stretched his neck, obviously reluctant to tell me. "McDonald's," he said eventually.

I laughed. "No way. Me too."

"Really?"

"Well, not any more. Back in Wellington."

"Was it okay down there?"

I shrugged. "Wouldn't have been so bad if I wasn't vegetarian."

Adam shook his head and rubbed his eyes, laughing.

"What?" I looked up at him.

"Nothing. Just ... me too."

I sat up. "Really? You're vegetarian?"

He nodded. "Pescatarian. But there's only so many fish burgers you can eat!"

I shook my head. "Freud would have a field day with our choice in careers."

I leaned back against Adam's shoulder and sipped my hot chocolate as we talked. It was easier now we had something other than dead parents in common. Before, it was always like he was a second away from asking. Now I could just distract him with horror stories of night shifts and cleaning the fryer.

I yawned as I felt my eyelids drooping. I could feel his breath slowing too, as he settled into the sleepiness of the place. The pattern of the fire was hypnotic, flickering and dancing until my eyes relaxed into a blur. I yawned again, and let my eyes close.

· · · ·

I WOKE WITH A START. The fire had died down, and there were only a few people left sitting around it.

"Hey, you drifted off for a bit." Adam shifted, moving his arm from around me. He flexed his hand, like it had gone numb.

"Sorry, that's so embarrassing." I pulled away from him and started bundling up Amber's blanket.

Adam chuckled. "Not a problem. Did you know you talk in your sleep, though?"

I glanced at Adam. He was laughing, so I couldn't have said anything awful. No screaming nightmares, at least.

"I should get back to the cabins," I said.

Adam frowned. "You don't have to. They make the curfew later on campfire night."

I shook my head. "No, I have to go. I shouldn't have stayed so late."

"But–"

I turned away from Adam and headed up the path back to the cabins. The end of Amber's blanket came loose and tangled around my legs. I threw it around my shoulders like a cape and kept going. I felt like running, letting it flow out behind me like a budget superhero. But my foot was prickling with pins and needles, so I had to settle for a limping jog instead.

I stopped when I reached the cabins, and glanced back as if Adam might be following me. That was hardly the most graceful exit. I should have explained about Tilly sleeping in my bed, so he knew it wasn't about him. But it's hard to act normal around someone when you've forced them into acting as your pillow. I just hoped I hadn't been drooling on his shoulder while I slept.

The light was off in Amber and Jenny's cabin, so I shook the blanket out and folded it up neatly. I couldn't tell if they were still at the campfire or if they'd gone to bed early. Either way, I'd return the blanket in the morning.

I stopped as I got to the steps of my cabin. There were voices – one male, one female – coming from close by. I froze. The trees beside the cabins rustled, and a bird above me let out a warning cry.

I relaxed as I heard laughing. Technically I supposed they weren't breaking any rules, since they weren't in either the boys' or the girls' cabins. I had a feeling rolling around in the bushes wasn't exactly what the staff had in mind as a compromise, though.

I shook my head and started up the steps.

I froze again as I heard Clare's voice. "See you later, yeah?"

There was more rustling, then she appeared out of the bushes. She stopped as she saw me. I saw the guy walking away.

Just a flash of a red T-shirt, and a tattoo on his arm below the end of his sleeve.

Clare eyed me, like she was considering turning tail. I tried to think of something reassuring to say. *Hey, we've all been caught in the bushes once or twice,* was all I could think of, and I didn't think that would go down too well. I attempted a smile instead.

Clare scowled and walked past me. I heard her cabin door slam from around the corner, and shook my head at the drama of it.

I turned on the light inside my cabin. Freya's bed was empty, the blankets on the floor where she'd dumped them that morning. There was a little mound under the covers in my bed. I sighed and turned off the light again.

"No nightmares tonight, please," I whispered, but I wasn't sure whether I meant me or Tilly. I went out to the bathroom to change into my pyjamas, then slipped into bed next to her.

Tilly stirred, shifting herself into the curve of my body. I couldn't tell whether she was awake, or if it had become so automatic now that she moved to fit against me without having to be conscious.

I brushed the hair off her face, and her eyelids fluttered under my hand. "I love you, Tilly," I said, and wrapped my arms around her.

Four

THE LAST THING I SAID to mum was, "Goodnight." I think people always obsess over that, whether their last words to someone meant something. I don't think it really did. It was what I said every night, more out of habit than anything else. Sometimes I was angry when I said it, usually over something totally stupid. Sometimes I really meant it; I really cared that she slept well, because I loved her and wanted her to know that.

The night she died, I think it was just neutral. A cursory thing I said for no other reason than custom.

• • • •

I SLEPT LATE THE MORNING after the campfire, only waking when Tilly kicked my shin as she clambered over me to go to the bathroom. I didn't want to get up, but after a moment I realised I needed to pee too, so I dragged myself out from under the covers.

Freya wasn't in her bed. I'd heard her come in last night, but I hadn't felt like talking so I'd pretended to be asleep while she crept around getting ready for bed.

I met Tilly in the bathroom, coming out of the stall. She pushed past me, hitting my hip with her shoulder on her way out.

"Careful, bub," I called after her, though I knew she hadn't done it accidentally.

I rubbed my eyes and stared at the graffiti on the toilet door. *"You are beautiful, inside and out. Never forget that."* I smiled. My ex told me the graffiti in girls' bathrooms is always nicer than the stuff written in the boys' loos. I decided it was best not to question how he knew that, but he was probably right.

I ran my hand over the wall then jerked it back, thinking of germs. Some of the graffiti had faded to the point of being unreadable, but other words looked like they'd been written yesterday. How many years had people been coming to Pine Hills and leaving their mark?

Someone had traced over some of the older ones with red pen, renewing them. "*Clare and Adam*" surrounded by a heart. I stared at it, then turned away.

When I came out of the bathroom, Tilly was back in bed with her head under the covers. Her toes were sticking out at the end of the bed. I thought about tickling them. It was tempting, but I remembered how much I used to hate it when Dad did that to me.

"Time to get up, Tilly," I said instead.

She shifted, drawing the blankets closer around herself.

"I know you're not asleep, Till." I pulled the covers off the bed. "Get up. You've got to go back to the kids' area."

Tilly rolled over, lying face down on the mattress. She tucked her elbows into the sides of her face, like she was warding off an attack. There were goosebumps rising on the backs of her arms, but I could tell she was determined not to move, even if she got cold.

I sighed and grabbed some clothes out of my bag. "I'm going to get dressed, and you'd better be up when I get back."

I couldn't help but laugh as I walked back into the bathroom. That was just the kind of threat Mum used to make too.

I never figured out what the end of it might be. I think I was always so scared of being told off, I'd get out of bed even without knowing what would happen if I didn't. But what would I do if I went back in and she wasn't up? I guessed I was about to find out.

Tilly was dressed and sitting on the side of the bed. I gave her a smile, but she refused to look at me.

"Ready to go back to the kids' area?" I asked.

She kicked the floor, making a loud thump.

"Come on," I said. "Or do I have throw you over my shoulder and drag you back there?"

Tilly stared at me, her face set into a scowl and her arms crossed. I hoped she didn't try me on that one. She was hard enough to carry when she was being compliant. If she were resisting me, it would be pretty near impossible.

Finally she gave an exaggerated sigh and stomped out of the room. She passed Freya in the doorway, and gave her a glare.

Freya held up her hands in surrender. "Whoa, what's up with you, Miss?"

Tilly tossed her head and didn't answer. Freya raised her eyebrows at me.

I shook my head. "She's fine, just in a strop."

I took Tilly's hand as we walked, but she shook me off. A moment later I felt her clinging to my pocket. I slowed my pace to let her keep up.

"When can we go home?" she asked.

I glanced down at her. "Don't you like it here, bub?"

She shrugged. "I want to go home." She scuffed her feet as she walked, making long skid marks behind her.

I sighed. "If you still feel like that in a couple of days, I'll talk to Gran, okay?"

She didn't answer, but she picked up her feet a little more as she walked.

The lady who'd walked Tilly back from the campfire was waiting for us at the play area. I felt my stomach tighten. No-one had questioned me about Tilly sleeping in my room so far, but surely they had to have noticed she wasn't sleeping in her own bed. I slowed my pace even further, wanting to delay facing the inevitable questions.

"There you are, Tilly!" The lady smiled, and held out her hand to me. "I'm Anne, one of the senior staff here."

I took her hand, shaking it briefly. She didn't seem like a senior anything. I didn't think she could be much older than me, and she was wearing an oversized plastic gum-ball ring on her ring finger. It cut into my palm as she squeezed my hand.

Tilly scowled at Anne and kicked at the dirt between them.

I flicked her arm. "Don't be rude, Tilly."

Tilly scowled at the ground instead. She muttered something under her breath; something that sounded very much like a string of swear words. I blushed. Mum had always told me off for swearing in front of Tilly, and I could see why now.

"Sorry," I said to Anne. "Till's in a bit of a bad mood this morning."

Anne smiled again, and crouched down to Tilly's level. "Jack was looking for you, Tilly. Why don't you go find him?"

Tilly swung her arms, not letting go of my pocket. I stroked the hair off her face, in the way Mum used to do to me when I was in a strop. I used to hate it when she did that. I think part of me liked it too, though, because then I felt I was justified in being annoyed at her, even if it wasn't actually her fault. Tilly groaned and pushed my hand away, just the way I used to. I pressed my lips together to stop myself from laughing at her. Suddenly she changed her mind and ran off.

"See you later, Till," I called after her.

She reached the jungle gym and started climbing. She climbed in the same way she ran – arms and legs going every-where. Jack was balanced on the top, waiting for her. I smiled as he reached down his hand to help her up the last little bit.

Anne stared after Tilly, then turned back to me. "You must be Bailey. Tilly's told me a lot about you."

I nodded. I wasn't sure if that was true. "Bailey's my sister" was the most anyone normally got out of her.

Anne started to walk, and after a moment I realised I was supposed to keep pace with her. I jogged a couple of steps to catch up, then slowed back to a walk.

"Tilly obviously thinks a lot of you," she said.

I shrugged. "We've always been pretty close." That wasn't true, either. There'd always been enough of an age gap between us that I felt more like Tilly's babysitter than her sister.

But Anne nodded. "And after everything that's happened, I suppose more so."

I stopped. The breeze seemed to rush in my ears, making the kids' voices sound further away. Anne turned back to face me. I stared over her shoulder. There was a group of birds be-hind her, fighting over a crust of bread. I had a childish urge to run at them, making them scatter in panic.

I swallowed, my mouth feeling thick. "How did you–?"

"I called your grandmother. I was concerned when Tilly kept disappearing to your room at night." Anne started walking again. After a couple of paces, I joined her. She twisted the ring as she moved, making the plastic gem glint in the sun with each step. Round and round and round, until I was sure she must be unscrewing her finger.

"I'd thought perhaps moving to the family units might be an idea," she said, "but your gran insisted this was the better option for you."

I felt my cheeks flush. No wonder Gran had been so worried when I went up to see her. I sniffed, and caught the scent of honeysuckle. We used to have that in the garden at home. Somewhere. We could always smell it in summer, but never found the plant. Sometimes I wondered if it was growing in the walls, just to make the house smell good.

I looked towards Anne, but still didn't quite meet her eye. "I'm sorry," I said finally. "I didn't realise." I shook my head.

Anne nodded gently to herself. "We're normally a lot stricter with this kind of thing," she said. "But we decided you and Tilly were a special case."

I swallowed, a heavy lump forming in my throat. I wondered how much Gran had told her. A little was probably enough, and there was no way I could go into details with a complete stranger.

"Bailey, there's something ..." Anne frowned. She picked some lint off her T-shirt then smoothed it out over the top of her shorts. She had an affected way of talking, like she was trying to sound older. But she faltered now, sounding just as young as she looked.

I waited, but it didn't seem like she was going to continue. "Something ...?"

She looked up at me and sighed. She pulled the picture of Mum and Dad, the one from my wall, out of her pocket. "We found this. In Tilly's bed."

I stared at the photo. Tilly had scribbled over it, black lines and swirls covering the background and their faces.

"I wasn't sure whether—"

I cut her off. "It's fine." My voice came out croaky and my throat burned. I felt my cheeks and eyes heating up too.

"I'm sorry. This must be very hard for you to deal with."

I wasn't sure whether she meant the photo or just everything. I stared back towards the playground. Tilly was hanging upside down again, her hair flying out around her, turning her into a mini-Medusa.

"She doesn't mean to ..." I took a breath. Tilly still had the Pooh Bear Band-Aid on her knee. It was turning grey around the edges, as the adhesive collected dirt and grime. I should have taken it off, or at least made her change it. But she'd squealed every time I got near it and I'd given up.

Anne touched my shoulder, leaving her hand pressed against my skin. I closed my eyes and searched in the back of my mind for the words Tilly's counsellor had used. "Post-traumatic stress disorder," I said. I didn't want to be angry with Tilly.

Anne leant forward as I mumbled it. I don't think she heard me, but I decided it didn't matter. It didn't actually explain anything more than common sense.

I raised my head and looked at Anne properly. "Thank you," I said. I slipped the photo into my pocket.

She nodded. She opened her mouth, but hesitated before continuing. Her lips held the stretched shape, turning her face into a gaping mask. "We do have counsellors available," she said finally. "If–"

"No." I shook my head, making my hair flap around me. "No, thank you." We'd tried that. Or Tilly had, at least. She wouldn't talk to them, and I didn't want to. I started to back away. "I have to go now," I said. I kept walking backwards for a few paces.

Anne's face was frozen into that mask. Her hair swirled around her, tossed by the breeze, but her face didn't change. I looked towards Tilly. She was upside down still. Her hands dangled, lifeless at the ends of her arms. Her whole body was swaying. Back and forth. Her hair swept the ground, like it was alive and she wasn't. I felt bile rise in my throat.

"See you later, Bailey," Anne called after me.

I started to run.

I ran all the way back to the cabins, letting the air rush against my face. Gravel flicked up against my legs, stinging them. I imagined it embedding itself in my skin, leaving me decorated with throbbing grey mounds. The image made me retch. I cut through the bush, covering the gravel welts with branch-scratches instead.

I stopped at the path to the girls' cabins, leaning against the archway. My breath made ugly wheezing noises as I tried to stop crying. Anne's mask-like face kept filling my head, frozen in that look of pity. It didn't matter what I did, there was always going to be someone wanting to talk, wanting to tell me they understood how I felt.

"I hate this place!" I said aloud.

"You're not the only one."

I jumped as Clare spoke. I turned away and rubbed my face, smearing away the evidence I'd been crying. Fat chance of that working, I thought.

I wanted to run again, to pretend I hadn't heard her and take off. But I made myself turn back towards her.

She was sitting beside the path, under a tree, camouflaged by the shade. She tipped her head to the side, watching me. "Talking to yourself?" She raised her eyebrows.

I shook my head and swallowed, trying to think of a sensible answer. "Must be getting heatstroke," I mumbled finally.

Clare nodded, then leaned back against the tree. She closed her eyes and I wondered if I could just slip away without her noticing. I squeezed my palms against my face as I felt another wave start inside me.

"Sit down, before it takes hold," Clare said, and opened one eye to look at me.

I hesitated. I just wanted to find a quiet hole where I could hide and cry alone. Instead I sat down next to her.

I rubbed my face again. My eyes must have been bloodshot. Even without the tears, I was very aware of how sweaty I was. Clare's skin was cool; I don't think I'd seen her perspire once in the entire time I'd been there.

It was a nice spot – sheltered, but not too cold. Most of the time, I'd felt like a lizard running back and forth between sun and shade, trying to control its temperature.

"I was being rude yesterday." Clare sniffed, and shifted her position against the tree. She glanced over at me. "I get a bit ... territorial." It wasn't quite an apology, but it was better than nothing.

I shrugged and took a couple of slow breaths, letting the calm of the place settle over me. We sat without speaking for a moment, bird calls and cicadas providing a soundtrack. Clare's hair was loose, splaying out and tickling my shoulder. I resisted the urge to flick it away.

"So, what's up with you?" Clare tilted her head to look at me. "Or do you always bawl your eyes out when you go for a run."

I sighed and leaned back against the tree. What could I say? There weren't enough lies in the world to make sense of this mess.

"Would you believe shin splints?" I said eventually.

Clare wrinkled her nose. "About as much as I believe that scar is from your appendix."

I stared at Clare. My eyes spilled over again, and I put my head in my hands. I didn't even try to disguise it, just letting myself cry openly.

Clare went quiet, then finally she shrugged. "It's okay, Bailey. We've all got secrets."

I nodded through the tears. I rubbed my face and tried to stop crying. Clare patted the ground beside her, then held out a leaf. When I didn't take it from her, she dropped it in my lap and shrugged.

"I don't have any tissues," she said. "It's the best I can do."

I stared at her, then laughed. "Thanks." I ran my finger over the spiky points of the leaf's edge. I contemplated actually wiping my face with it, then decided against it as it started to crumble, dry under my touch. I dropped it on the path next to me instead. As soon as I did, a ridiculous level of sentimentality took over and I wanted to grab it back. To press it in a book as memento of the trip. Or perhaps a memento of Clare actually being nice.

"Speaking of secrets," Clare glanced over at me, "I'd really rather no-one else found out about what you saw me doing the other night."

I looked up at her. I wasn't sure what she was talking about at first, then I shook my head. "I didn't see anything really, just—"

"Just me in the bushes with Josh. You're not an idiot, Bailey. You saw enough."

I hesitated, then nodded. "I didn't know it was Josh, but yeah." I wondered what Clare's secrets were, other than private rendezvous with guys in the bushes, and if there was any point in asking.

"Anyway, I don't want anyone to know." Clare cleared her throat. "Especially Adam, so—"

I nodded. "Of course. I won't say anything."

Clare looked away. I felt a lump in my throat as I realised she was close to tears herself. I thought of the heart on the bathroom wall, binding her and Adam's names together.

"Clare, I ..." I held my breath, wondering if I was just digging a deeper hole. "There's nothing going on between me and Adam," I said finally.

I felt her hair shift against me, with the rise and fall of her breath. Her lips made a sticky sound as they parted, but she didn't speak.

"That first day, he was just helping me out with Tilly," I said. "And yesterday ..." I shrugged. I wasn't sure what yesterday was. "I'm not interested in him. Really."

I wanted to face Clare as I said that, but it was too awkward.

She made a sound that was almost a laugh. "What *have* Amber and Jenny been saying?"

"Nothing. Just that you used to be together."

"So you think I'm going to scratch your eyes out for hanging out with him?" There was a nasty edge to Clare's voice. *Yeah*, I wanted to say. *It wouldn't surprise me.*

"Look," I said instead. "I just know how I felt when my ex started dating again, and–"

"He dumped you?" She turned to face me, her eyes widening with voyeuristic interest.

I pressed my lips together. I hadn't meant to say anything about David; I hadn't meant to tell her *anything*.

"It was complicated," I said eventually.

She wrinkled her nose, obviously not considering that an answer. "And it's not, when?"

I stood up. "I just meant that you don't have to worry about me. If you're not over him."

Clare shrugged like she couldn't care less. I rolled my eyes and turned away. I didn't have the energy to play matchmaker, especially if she was going to act like it didn't matter.

"I dumped him, in case you're wondering," Clare called after me.

I looked back over my shoulder at her. "Yeah?"

She gave me a half-smile. "It's never that simple, though, is it?"

· · · ·

BY THE EVENING, THE water was calling me again. I took Tilly with me to the pool this time. It worried me too much, leaving her, knowing she'd probably follow. I lifted her over the fence and she settled down on one of the loungers with some paper and a felt tip pen.

"Having fun, Tilly?" I called to her between lengths.

"I'm okay," she said.

I dived again and swam a few more lengths. When I surfaced, she was sitting on the side of the pool, dangling her feet in the water.

"You had enough, bub?" I pulled myself out and sat beside her.

She shrugged. "It's getting cold."

"That's because your feet are wet." I rubbed them with my towel, then wrapped it around myself as she put her sandals back on.

"Why do you only swim at night?"

I squeezed the water from my hair. "I told you. It's too busy during the day."

Tilly frowned, and I could see that ticking over in her brain. "It's because of your scars, isn't it?"

I sighed. "Till–"

"Gran says you shouldn't be ashamed of them." She stared at me, her eyes wide and solemn.

I looked out over the surface of the water. A breeze picked up, making it ripple in dark, inky swirls. I wanted to dive back in and feel the water rush against my skin.

I picked up one of Tilly's drawings. The felt tip pen bled under my wet hands.

"Why did you draw on the photo, Till?" I didn't look at her as I asked the question, but forced myself to when she didn't answer. "I'm not angry," I said, though it wasn't entirely true. "I just want to know."

Tilly fiddled with the buckle on her sandal, bending it back and forth. The metal tooth made little clicks as it tapped against the square clip. They were jelly sandals, the kind with glitter set in them. But in the dark they didn't sparkle.

I knelt down and did up the buckle for her. She didn't look at me, but I felt her arm pressing against mine.

"Come on," I said. "You'll freeze if you stay out here."

I went to lift Tilly back over the fence, but she pushed me away. "I can do it!" She gripped the top of the fence, pulled herself up then scrambled down the other side without even having to think about it. I smiled. Playing on the jungle gym was giving her more confidence, even if she still looked unco-ordinated doing everything. My towel slid off as I climbed over myself.

"Wouldn't have picked you as a rule breaker, Bailey." Adam's voice rang out of the dark as I dropped down on the other side.

I wrapped the towel back around me and squinted at the path. "I know. I'm full of surprises."

I could just make out Adam's silhouette as he walked towards me. His head seemed far bigger than it should have. "What are you ...?"

He flicked on the torch from his cell phone. "Kids' craft day. Jack made me this hat."

I opened my mouth, but couldn't think what to say. Jack's hat was a tower of fluoro-green paper curls. The effect was somewhere between judge's wig and Marge Simpson.

Adam raised his eyebrows. "Stunning, isn't it?"

I pressed my lips together to stop myself laughing. "Indeed. Stunning."

I glanced down at Tilly. She swung her arms on the spot and stared at the ground. I don't think she'd even noticed what Adam was wearing.

I picked her up. "Come on. I need to get this one to bed."

"I'll walk you back to the cabins."

It was difficult, balancing Tilly and trying to keep my towel from dropping off. I set her down after only a few paces. No matter how I wound the ends of the towel together, they still came loose in a matter of seconds.

Adam paused beside me as I struggled with it. "How about a piggyback, Tilly?"

She stared at him, not quite willing to commit.

"Go on, Tilly," I said. "I bet Adam gives Jack piggybacks all the time."

He grinned at me and ducked down so that Tilly could climb up. She tucked her head against his shoulder and closed her eyes. I'd have to remember not to keep her out so late, she was asleep on her feet.

"So, do you always go swimming at midnight?"

I shrugged. "Only on the full moon." I remembered then, that I wasn't supposed to be able to swim at all. I waited for Adam to ask me, but he didn't. He didn't seem like the type to pry, so I was probably safe with him knowing I was lying.

We didn't talk much on the walk back. It was okay, though. It was kind of like that first day, when I saw him sitting across the pool. A moment of quiet in all the frenetic energy of this place.

Adam stopped at the path to the girls' cabins.

I raised my eyebrows. "Not a rule-breaker?"

He laughed. "Not tonight."

His face went serious for a moment, then he was back to the frown that wasn't really a frown. "I'm glad you came yesterday, Bailey."

"To the pool party?" I laughed. "Between you and Gran, I didn't have much of a choice."

He looked up at me, sharply. "Wouldn't you have–?"

"No, I didn't mean it like that. Sorry."

There was a silence, but this time not a comfortable one. I cursed myself for being so rude. He didn't need to know I was avoiding people, especially after he'd been so kind to me and Tilly.

"Bailey–"

"I'm sorry–" I stopped as we both started talking at once.

He hesitated, then gave that goofy smile. "There you go, apologising again."

I laughed and shook my head. "I know; I've got to stop doing that."

He reached out, touching my face and making me look at him. I froze, his hand warm against my cold skin.

"Bailey–"

Movement beside us cut him off. Someone running back towards the cabins. I stepped back, making him drop his hand.

"Was that …?" He peered down the path. I don't think he'd seen who it was, but I had.

"I'd better get Tilly to bed." I lifted her from him and started down the path.

"See you tomorrow, Bailey?"

I turned my head to show I'd heard, but didn't answer.

Five

SOMETIMES I THINK memories are like being underwater. You can see the real world, the current world, but it's so remote you don't feel connected to it.

Dad said that's what he thought I liked about swimming, the fact that I could cut myself off. He was mad at me when he said it – I don't remember why. Something about me not wanting to hang out with him and Mum all day.

I went down to the pool early the next morning. It seemed a fair bet that Clare would be there. Even though I'd never seen her actually get in the water, she spent nearly every waking moment on a sun lounger beside the pool.

She didn't look up as I opened the gate, but I could tell she'd noticed me. Her posture was pretend-relaxed, but every muscle in her body was tense.

I sat down on the lounger next to her. "Clare–"

She picked up a magazine from the ground beside her, and buried her face in it.

I sighed. "I meant what I said yesterday. I'm not interested in Adam."

Clare raised her eyebrows, above her sunglasses. I'd never seen her take the slightest care to be sun smart. In fact her arms had turned a toffee colour, and her shoulders were flaking where the skin had burnt. My guess would be the sunglasses were to hide red eyes. She made a little noise in her throat, and turned a page.

I shook my head. "It's true. I'm not interested in any guys at the moment."

"So what, you're gay now? Been hanging out with Amber and Jenny too much?"

I hesitated, confused. Amber and Jenny were a couple? I guess I wasn't really all that surprised. The gentle affection between them, the way they smiled when they met each other's eye – it all felt so natural. They seemed to fit.

That didn't make it okay for Clare to go around telling people, though. Suddenly Amber and Jenny's weirdness around Clare made sense. Clare was a stroppy little bully through and through.

I shook my head. "Clare ... if you want to get back together with Adam, then–"

"Then what?" Clare sat up. "I should go begging him to take me back?" She shook her head. "He probably told you he broke up with me, didn't he? I bet you had a good laugh about it." Clare stood. I fumbled as I tried to stand and back away. She was leaning over me now, yelling, and I felt myself shrink.

"He tell you why? Apparently, I'm too selfish and manipulative." She laughed. "How do you think he feels about liars, Little Miss I-can't-swim?"

I looked up at her. She stared down at me with a smirk. "It's amazing what you can find out on Google these days, Bailey."

I stared back. Google. Did she just mean the swimming, or had she found out about everything else? My throat hurt with the words I was holding back. I wanted to tell her I'd been trying to help – that even if I had been interested in Adam, I would have stepped aside for her. I wanted to tell her none of it was any of her business. If she thought it was okay to use that against me, then Adam was right. She was manipulative and selfish.

"What were you doing in the bushes last night?" I remembered that first night, when I'd thought someone was watching me and Tilly at the pool.

Clare laughed. "Afraid of what else I might have seen? What have you been doing, Bailey?"

I got up and pushed her away. "Just leave me alone, you ..." I shook my head, frustrated at the tears swallowing my voice. "Just leave me alone."

I ran back to my cabin. Running was almost as good as swimming. The air rushed in my ears, turning the world into a pulsing, whooshing sound. My arms and legs burned, and my attention turned to the heat in my cheeks.

I didn't want to stop. I wanted to just keep going – to let my head pound with exertion rather than anger, but Tilly would be waking soon and I needed to be there.

I grabbed my towel from the cabin, then jumped in the shower next door. The water pouring over my head blocked out the worst of the noise in my thoughts. I turned the temperature up until it stung at my skin.

Freya was waiting for me when I got out. She chewed on her lip as she greeted me at the door. "Bailey, something's wrong with–"

"Where is she?" I didn't wait for Freya to answer. I could tell from her face what had happened.

The floor of the cabin was littered with paper. Tilly had torn up her drawings, scribbling over the scraps until they went from being patterns to just a mess of colours.

I opened the door to the wardrobe. Tilly lay on her side, her arms shielding her head.

"How long?" I looked at Freya.

She shook her head. "I don't know. I woke up and she was in here. What's wrong with her?"

I just shook my head. I climbed into the wardrobe with Tilly and wrapped my arms around her. "Tilly? Tilly, it's all right. You can come out now."

I took Tilly up to Gran's rather than leaving her at the playground. She tucked Tilly up on the couch, then asked if I wanted to stay too. I shook my head, said I had to go talk to someone. She gave me a knowing look, and made some comment about "young love". I didn't have the energy to explain I didn't mean Adam, and that with all his and Clare's history there was very little chance of love of any kind. Instead I just nodded and let her think what she wanted.

Amber and Jenny's door was open when I got back to the cabins. I could see them both dancing around with their headphones on, and Jenny singing into a hairbrush. Her voice was pretty good, but I'm not sure she realised how loud she was. I don't think they were listening to the same song, as Amber was dancing to a totally different rhythm. Only Jenny was singing, though, so it was hard to say for sure.

I knocked on the door to get their attention. "Hello?"

Jenny grabbed my hands and pulled me into the room. "Dance with us, Bailey." She was shouting at the top of her lungs, even louder than her singing had been.

I reached forward to take her headphones off. "Can I –?"

"What?"

I mimed taking off the headphones to her and Amber.

Amber pulled hers out. "Sorry. What's up?" She turned the player on her phone off, then wound the headphones around it and put it in her pocket. Jenny started doing the same but got the cable tangled. Somehow it managed to wind itself around the button on her pocket, and got caught on her bracelet at the same time.

Amber laughed. "You're so unco-ordinated, Jenny."

Jenny poked her tongue out at her. "It's the pocket goblins, I swear!"

I hovered while Amber made an attempt at freeing Jenny. "I just ..." I wasn't quite sure how to phrase what I wanted to say, especially with them both distracted in untangling the cable. "I don't really ..."

"Spit it out, Bailey." Amber grinned at me. She pulled one of Jenny's curls, making it spring back towards Jenny's head. Jenny laughed and slapped her hand away. They were both wearing pink sparkly nail polish, which reminded me of Tilly's sandals.

I sighed and rubbed my face. "Look it's just, Clare said some stuff this morning and–"

"What kind of stuff?" Amber stopped what she was doing, her hand frozen, hovering over Jenny's hair. Her forehead was slowly creasing into a frown, but Jenny just shrugged.

She stared at Amber, not me, as she spoke. "She told you we're together, didn't she?"

"Jenny!" Amber looked from me to Jenny. I couldn't tell whether she was going to cry, or yell at one of us. Or maybe both. Her chest rose and fell faster, as her breath quickened. I felt mine do the same, drawing the panic from her. I had to fight the urge to turn and run.

"I mean, it doesn't make a difference to me, you know?" I hurried through the thoughts I'd gathered together on my run.

"But I figured if you'd wanted me to know you would have told me yourselves, and–"

"Too late for that now, isn't it?" Amber turned away from me. I swallowed and picked at the seam on my shorts. It was coming unstitched, little threads creeping out to greet my fingers. I pulled at them, making the seam come undone faster.

"Amber, I–"

She walked out, cutting me off. I stared at Jenny, wishing I'd just stayed at Gran's. Jenny wrinkled her nose, then flinched as we heard the bathroom door slam. She sat down on the bed and rubbed her face.

I hovered beside her, unsure whether to stay or go. "I'm sorry," I said eventually. "I shouldn't have said anything."

Jenny shrugged. "It's not your fault. *Clare's* the one who shouldn't have said anything; you were just trying to be a good friend." She flopped back on the bed, turning herself into a human starfish.

We weren't really friends, though. I barely knew any of these people, and yet somehow I was still getting caught up in all their drama. But Jenny and Amber did seem like nice people. Nicer than Clare, at any rate.

Jenny raised her head to look at me. "Sit down, you're making me nervous."

I perched on the edge of the bed. I'm fairly sure I looked more awkward sitting than standing. Jenny rolled over onto her stomach and went back to trying to untangle her headphones, so she didn't notice.

"Did Amber tell you she and Clare used to be best friends?" Jenny looked back over her shoulder at me.

I shook my head. Amber hadn't really said anything about Clare, other than the stuff about Adam. Even that was the abbreviated version, I was sure.

Jenny nodded to herself. "They go to the same school, back home. Amber's family only started coming here because Clare's parents recommended it." Jenny rubbed her tongue against her teeth, scrunching up her face. She glanced up at me again. "Most of us only see each other once a year, but Amber and Clare see each other nearly every day."

I made a face. "So that makes it okay for Clare to act like a cow?"

Jenny laughed. "Of course not, it makes it worse. It's just ..." She shook her head. Her tone was more hesitant when she continued. "Amber says Clare's different at home. Like, nicer and stuff."

I couldn't really see it myself. I'd only been here a few days, and even in that time I could tell you never knew where you stood with Clare. It was obvious she could be vicious when she wanted to be.

Jenny shrugged. "I don't really believe it. They go to one of those super strict private schools, so I think she's probably just better at hiding her mess."

Jenny dumped the headphones down on the bed, admitting defeat, and flopped her head down on the pillow. She watched me, squinting as she tried to make her eyes focus side on.

I picked up the headphones and had a go at unwinding them myself. It was strangely methodical, like a meditation or an exercise in patience.

"So I'm guessing no-one else knows about you two?" I asked.

Jenny made a noise in her throat. "It's complicated."

"When is it not?" I groaned, realising I was practically quoting Clare.

Jenny stared at me, like she was trying to suss me out. I did my best to look trustworthy.

Finally she nodded. "My parents know, but Amber's don't. They're kind of religious ..." She rubbed her temple. "It'll be fine, but Amber's not ready to deal with it yet."

"And Clare knows all this?" I felt my cheeks heating up. It was bad enough she wanted to mess around in my life, but I couldn't believe she'd do that to someone who considered her a friend.

Jenny forced a smile. "Just don't get on Clare's bad side, is all I can say."

I shook my head. "Too late."

I heard the bathroom door open, and Amber's steps on the deck. She faltered outside the door. I wondered if I should go. Perhaps she was hovering, trying to see if I was still hanging around. I stood up as she came back in.

"How you doing, Babe?" Jenny rolled onto her back, propping herself up on her elbows.

Amber waved Jenny's question away and turned to me. "We're going down to the pool, you want to come?"

I didn't want to. Really, I just wanted to get back up to Gran's and check on Tilly. Amber bit her lip, and I realised she wanted me to act as a Clare-buffer.

"Sure," I said.

• • • •

AS SOON AS I OPENED the gate, I could see something was wrong. Adam and Clare were on the other side of the pool, arguing. I took a step towards them.

Amber caught my arm. "I wouldn't, if I were you."

I glanced at her. "What do you think's going on?"

She shrugged. "Over-reaction of epic proportions, would be my guess." She slipped her sunglasses down from her forehead. "Don't get involved."

I looked back across the pool. Adam was holding Clare's phone and gesturing at it with angry fingers. He turned towards me and met my eye. His face fell into a surprised frown. Clare smirked at me.

"Don't get involved," I repeated to myself. I turned away.

"Bailey!" Adam called, making me look back. He shoved the phone at Clare. She fumbled, nearly dropping it in the water. I stopped as Adam ran to catch up with me.

He glanced back at Clare. "There's a teddy bear's picnic on today. Do you want to take Jack and Tilly?" His tone was urgent and his hands fidgeted at his sides.

I frowned and looked back at Clare too. She stared at me from across the pool.

"What's going on?" I asked Adam.

"Huh?" He was staring at Clare again. He tore his focus back to me. "No, nothing. Nothing." He forced a smile. "We just ..." His face darkened and he lowered his voice. "We shouldn't stay here today, okay?"

My chest felt tight. Clare was walking towards me.

"Bailey ..." Adam shook his head. His eyes were crinkling up into worried slits.

I backed away. "I'm sorry. This is just too–" My foot slipped on the edge of the pool. I threw my arms up, but it was too late.

Amber screamed as I fell. "She can't swim!"

The crash as my back hit the water knocked the air out of me. My nose and mouth filled with water, and for the first time in my life I was sinking.

I remembered my dream, in which I sank to the pool floor, drowning, only to be saved by growing gills and a tail. I watched my feet floating in front of me. I waited for them to grow green and shiny with scales.

Someone dived in beside me, and that snapped me out of it. I righted myself and pushed towards the surface. My clothes weighed me down, and instinct took over. I pulled them off and kicked, like I'd been trained to do.

I broke into the air, coughing up the water I'd swallowed. Someone grabbed my arms and pulled me out. I opened my eyes and realised everyone was standing staring at me.

"Why'd you say you can't swim?" Jenny laughed, then her face changed as she looked at my stomach. "Oh my god, how'd you get that scar?"

"Shut up, Jenny!" Amber knelt down next to me. "Are you okay, Bailey?"

I sat up, my head pounding. "Yeah, I'm–"

"Yeah, Bailey's fine." Clare stepped forward. "The knife just slipped when she was stabbing her parents."

My breath caught in my chest, sending pain through my body. "Clare ..." I stared at her. She met my eye and shook her head.

"Why don't you tell them about it, Bailey? Tell them how you've been lying to everyone since you got here." She gave a sharp laugh. "Or are you going to stick to your stupid appendix story?"

Her face dissolved as my eyes spilled over. I got up and ran.

· · · ·

I REMEMBER GOING INTO the kitchen. Maybe to get some water, but I'm not entirely sure. I think I'd forgotten by then, that I was supposed to be looking for Tilly, or maybe I'd just decided that it didn't matter so much. That if she was sleep walking she'd either wake up and go back to bed, or she'd fall properly asleep on the couch or the floor, and stay there until morning.

I turned on the kitchen light. It glinted against the broken glass on the floor. I thought it was a smashed dish at first, then I felt the draught and saw the shattered pane in the back door.

"Mum?" I called.

She didn't answer. I stepped towards the door and it swung free, the lock forced.

"Mum!" I yelled. "Mum, someone's broken the—"

I heard footsteps running down the stairs.

"Dad?"

Then there was more noise. More than one set of footsteps. And Dad yelling.

A man ran into the kitchen. I screamed. I ran for the door, but my feet were bare and the floor was covered in glass.

He grabbed me. I felt the knife in my side, but I didn't realise what it was. It didn't hurt; it was just a pressure, like he'd shoved me with his bare hand.

He let go of my arm and backed away. He dropped the knife. It clattered as it hit the floor, sending bits of glass bouncing away. I stared at his hands, held up in front of him like he was surrendering. I could see the blood, but I didn't realise it was mine.

I remember that it still didn't hurt, but that I felt dizzy. So dizzy, and like I was going to vomit.

I saw him run for the door. Someone else ran past me too, but I was staring at my hand. My hand on my side, and the red that was creeping out between my fingers. I looked up. I remembered that I was supposed to be looking for Tilly, but I was so dizzy. I took a step towards the door, but the floor didn't seem solid anymore.

I fell forward, landing face down in the pile of glass.

Six

I RAN FROM THE POOL until my head pounded and my eyes streamed. My foot caught on a root and I tripped.

I lay on my side on the ground. The earth was warm and damp. The smell of plants, and dirt, and insects surrounding me. I buried myself in it. If I lay here for long enough, would the earth just naturally cover me? Would the plants grow up around me until I completely disappeared?

In my dreams, I'm stuck on the floor in the kitchen, and the ceiling's caving in. I try to pull myself out, but I'm buried.

I heard someone walking towards me, but I didn't move. I was shaking still, and couldn't face talking to anyone.

I felt someone sit down next to me, then a towel being laid over me.

"Don't get cold." Adam's voice was soft.

I turned my face away. "I didn't stab my parents."

He settled back against a tree trunk. "I know."

I swallowed and closed my eyes. My chest ached with the scream I was keeping inside. "Clare–"

"Clare's an idiot who likes to mess with other people's feelings." He cleared his throat. "No-one's stupid enough to believe the rubbish she says." He pulled at the grass beside him, picking at the blades. "She did find some stuff online, though."

I pressed my hands against my mouth, feeling like I was going to vomit. All the awful things people had said flooded back – that I was involved, that Dad was a criminal, drugs. No-one wanted to believe we were just unlucky. "Most of that stuff–"

"I know. There's a load of rubbish on the internet." He shifted. "Is it how you got those scars, though?"

I nodded. He'd said *scars*, plural, so they'd all seen the ones on my face too. Not that they would have stayed hidden for much longer, anyway. There's only so long you can hide behind hair before everything gets exposed.

Adam didn't say anything. I knew what he was trying to tell me. If I wanted to talk about it, he'd listen. But I didn't have to.

What could I say? I'd never been able to say most of it out loud. None of the details, anyway.

"I don't remember much of what happened," I said. That was the excuse I'd used to not go to therapy too. How could I talk about it, if I didn't remember what happened?

Adam nodded. "Clare said a home invasion?"

"Yeah." The description seemed to fall flat. *Robbery gone wrong*, was what the police called it. "They were looking for money, but ..." But instead they killed my parents and left me for dead. "They never found the guys that did it. Tilly never saw them and I couldn't remember anything." That wasn't true. I remembered so much of that night, but none of the right bits. The thing I remember most was the glass. I could tell you exactly where every piece lay, but that was no help to the police.

Maybe I saw the guy who stabbed me. If I had, I'd blocked it out. When I woke up in the hospital later, there was just a blank space where his face should have been.

"It's not your fault, Bailey."

I closed my eyes again. There was stuff he couldn't possibly know – stuff I didn't even tell the police. They broke the glass in the back door with a garden trowel. Mum had asked me to weed the flower beds, and I didn't because I had training and because I'd had a fight with David and was too busy sulking.

She'd left the trowel on the doorstep, to remind me. I saw it there but pretended I didn't, and three nights later when they broke in it was still there.

"My dad was killed by a drunk driver, did I tell you that?"

I looked up at Adam. "You just said he died."

He stared straight ahead, frowning. "They caught the driver. He went to jail for two years." Adam shrugged. "It didn't really make a difference, you know? Whether he was charged or not, my dad was still dead."

I swallowed. I knew what he was trying to say, but it wasn't the same thing. Everyone always reassured me that it was unlikely the killers would come after Tilly and me – the police didn't think they'd intended to hurt anyone in the first place. But there would always be that outside possibility. I didn't know if I would ever feel safe again, ever able to stop looking over my shoulder.

Adam shook his head. "Clare ... she's not a bad person, you know?" He met my eye. "She just ... she does such stupid things." His jaw clenched as he said that.

I looked away. "I don't want to talk about Clare." I could tell he was angry with her – frustrated, and hurt, and a whole load of other things I couldn't even understand.

"It's over between us," he said, though it seemed to be more to himself than to me.

• • • •

JENNY, AMBER AND FREYA were waiting for me when I got back to the cabin. I didn't know what to say to them. They sat on Freya's bed in a line, like three wise monkeys.

"Adam called Clare a bitch after you left, and she's been locked in her cabin crying ever since," Jenny said.

I shook my head. "Am I supposed to feel sorry for her?"

Amber raised her eyebrows. "No, not in the least. We just thought you might enjoy the fact that she's suffering."

"I couldn't care less about Clare." I lay down on my bed and pulled the pillow over my head.

Jenny bounced on the mattress next to me. "What about Adam?"

I shook my head into the pillow and groaned. Jenny made a clucking noise with her tongue. I heard the muffled sound of the other girls shifting, through the pillow. They were having some kind of non-verbal conversation above me, I could tell.

They deserved a proper explanation, really. But I couldn't face it. I remembered what it was like, when my friends back home first came to visit me after it all happened. They tried so hard to be supportive and understanding. I could see how un-comfortable they were, though – how much they all wanted to escape.

"I'm sorry I lied before." I lifted the pillow a crack and peered out. "About the swimming."

Amber waved the apology away. "Dude, if that's the worst lie you've told, you're doing better than me."

"I'd figured it out anyway." Freya laughed. "I mean, it was kind of obvious when you kept coming in soaking wet."

I gave her a half-hearted smile. My hair was wet from the pool now, and I was still wearing Adam's towel. I got up and rummaged in my suitcase for some dry clothes.

"It's just ... it's hard to talk about." I pulled a T-shirt over my head and let the towel drop to the floor. "And when people see the scars, they want to know."

But the thing was, they didn't *really* want to know. They wanted the story, the gory details. Then they didn't know what to say, and things got weird. Because people can't handle knowing something like that happened to someone real, not just to characters on TV.

Jenny nodded. "And then you get loudmouths like me, who point them out to everyone."

I shook my head. "No, it's fine." I looked up at her. She chewed on her lip as she stared at me. "It wasn't your fault," I added.

She let out a breath. "Sorry, anyway. I always put my foot in it. I swear, if Amber wasn't here to stop me, then–"

"Babe." Amber tapped Jenny with her foot, and Jenny grinned.

"You see?"

I shook my head. "It's fine. Honestly." I leant down to pick up the towel. It was sopping wet from my hair, and left a damp patch on the floor. I spread it out, and then folded it up again, making a neat square. "Freya, could you give this back to Adam?" I tried to hand her the towel, but she didn't take it.

"Bailey–"

I shook my head. "I know what you're going to say, but I can't. I ..." I covered my face as it all came back again. Everyone had seen the scars. Everyone knew what had happened. Adam would just see me as a charity case now. "I just can't."

"Aw, sweetie ..." Amber wrapped her arms around me. "It's okay."

I didn't want to cry again, but I could feel it starting. Amber rubbed my back, and I felt the other girls come in close too.

"He was so nice about it, but ..." I remembered my friends back home, and the way they slowly drifted away. I remembered David at the airport, as he tried to look sad that I was leaving to go live with Gran, but really he just looked relieved.

"Of course he was nice about it!" Jenny said. "He likes you, Bailey."

"Not like that, he doesn't."

"You sure about that?"

I shook my head. Whatever he felt for me, he felt more for Clare. "It doesn't matter," I said instead. "He won't want to be around me now."

Jenny frowned. "Adam's not like that, Bailey. He's a nice guy."

"So was my ex," I said. Or at least David had been nice until everything happened. Then he was just a guy.

Freya shrugged. "Sounds like your ex was a dick."

Amber and Jenny looked at Freya then at each other. I could tell they'd both been thinking the same thing.

"No, he just ..." I trailed off. I didn't have to defend him now; we weren't together anymore. "He's dating my best friend now," I said instead. "We never actually broke up, but I left and ..." I swallowed. "It doesn't matter." I sat down on the floor again. Freya had picked up all the bits of Tilly's drawings and put them in the bin. I pulled one out. Bleed marks covered the edges, from where I'd touched them without drying my hands.

Jenny sat down on the floor next to me. She took the paper out of my hands and put it back in the bin. "Sounds like your friend was a dick too," she said.

"No, she ..." I stared at Jenny and the other girls, then started to laugh. "Yeah. Maybe."

I smoothed the T-shirt over my stomach. I was being a bit unfair to David, really. If the whole thing hadn't happened, we probably would have broken up anyway. We'd been on the verge of it for weeks. Relationships could get gory too, though, and talking about David was keeping them from asking about everything else.

Amber touched Jenny's arm. She nodded towards the door and lowered her voice. "Come on, we should let her get changed."

I smiled at Amber, realising she was giving me a chance to avoid any more questions.

"I left your clothes in the bathroom," she said, pulling Jenny away.

"Thanks."

I wanted to climb into bed and pull the duvet up over my head, but I had to go get Tilly from Gran's. Freya offered to make my bed for me while I went for a shower. I wasn't sure what she meant, until I realised lying down on it soaking wet hadn't been my smartest idea.

She grinned as she produced some spare bedding from the cupboard. "We've all done it at least once."

I nodded. "Thanks."

I flicked on the light in the bathroom. My T-shirt and shorts were hanging in one of the shower stalls. I took them down, squeezing out some of the excess water, and then rehung them on the back of the bathroom door. I turned the shower on and let it heat up.

I must have looked pretty strange, throwing off my clothes in the middle of the pool. My coach used to make us do drills, where we had to get in the pool fully dressed. I'd never realised until then how much extra fabric weighs when wet. How much it slows you down.

I stripped off and got in the shower. There was a plastic bag hanging from the towel hook in the stall. I glanced over my shoulder, as if the owner might be hovering beside me, then took the bag down. There was a swimsuit inside. I touched it, expecting it to be damp, forgotten after a trip to the pool, but it was dry.

Then I noticed a folded note pinned to the side of the bag, with my name scribbled on it. I unpinned it but it slipped from my hand, landing in the water pooled around my feet. I craned my neck, trying to catch the words before the water dissolved the ink completely.

Bails,

Thought this might help. It's a spare, so you can hang on to it.
Amber xx

I grinned as I shook out the swimsuit. It was a one-piece.

MY MUM AND DAVID'S mum were friends. Sometimes I think that's really all there was to our relationship. It hurt when I found out he was dating my best friend, but there was also a feeling of resignation to it, like I was relieved that I finally knew where I stood.

The night before I left to go to Gran's, I'd gone round to his house. I'd had to wait until Tilly was asleep, so I was late.

He was on the phone when I arrived. I saw him wince as he looked up at the cuts still raw on my face, and the way his eyes flicked away from me for the rest of the night. In hindsight, I knew it was over then.

. . . .

"SO ...?" JENNY LOWERED her voice, on the pretence of not waking Tilly. I think she just wanted to sound more dramatic, though. "Anything *interesting* happen today?"

We were sitting on the floor of her and Amber's cabin, eating a mix of marshmallows, scroggin and rice crackers. We'd all been getting a bit low on supplies, and had decided to pool our resources. Tilly was asleep on my bed, next door, but I'd left the doors open so I could hear if she woke up.

Jenny directed her question to all of us, but Amber and Freya both looked at me.

I rolled my eyes. "We hung out with Jack and Tilly at the kids' playground. You couldn't get more platonic if you tried."

Amber snorted. "Boring. What about you?" She looked at Freya.

Freya opened her mouth, surprised at Amber addressing her, and adjusted her glasses. She hung out with us all the time now, but I think she still felt like she was just there as my roommate.

"Yeah, we saw you sneaking off with that gorgeous-looking guy from the kitchen," Jenny added.

Freya blushed. "Hardly. That was the chef, and I was helping him bring in the bread delivery."

"You two are useless." Amber threw her hands up in mock-desperation. "How do you expect us to live vicariously through this snooze-fest?"

I laughed. Personally I didn't think she and Jenny needed to live vicariously through anyone. Jenny leaned her head against Amber's shoulder as we talked. They'd been a lot more relaxed since Clare outed them – at least around me. Freya hadn't said anything, but I think she'd probably figured it out too.

There were footsteps on the deck outside – flip-flops slapping back against bare soles. Jenny sat upright, jerking away from Amber. The steps faltered outside our door. Jenny craned her neck, peering around the doorframe to see who it was, then she made a face at me.

"Hey, thought I might find you in here." Clare came in and sat down. She didn't seem to realise we'd all heard her hovering outside.

I dropped my gaze, refusing to look at her. I didn't look up at the other girls, but I could feel them doing the same. Tiny changes in body language, allowing them to disengage.

Out of the corner of my eye, I saw Clare fidget as she settled herself on the floor across from me. There was no way she was oblivious to the mood in the room. The sound of our combined breathing swelled in the conversation void, until it seemed to fill the room like a liquid.

If I'd been in a charitable mood I would have started an argument with Clare, so we could thrash it all out and move on. Instead I let her squirm in the silence.

Jenny cleared her throat. "We were just thinking of heading to bed, so ..." She tilted her head towards the door.

Clare ignored the hint. Instead her hand jerked forward, grabbing a handful of Freya's scroggin. I looked up, startled by the movement. Clare met my eye for a second, then she did this weird twitchy thing with her chin and looked down at the nuts in her hand. There was something unnatural about her movements, like she was trying to pretend she wasn't drunk.

Jenny widened her eyes at me, her expression spelling out the exasperation we were all feeling. If it hadn't been for Amber, she'd probably have told Clare to piss off.

"Ugh, I hate raisins," Clare said, and chucked one back into the bag. It bounced out again, hit Jenny's thigh, then landed on the floor next to her.

I turned my head slowly, forcing my focus from Clare to the Houdini-raisin. Jenny stared at it, then shrugged and popped it in her mouth.

"Gross. You're such a scavenger." Amber grinned at her.

Jenny shrugged. "Waste not, want not."

Clare rolled her eyes. "Always after other people's castoffs, aren't you, Jenny?"

Jenny frowned and glanced at Amber. Amber shook her head, obviously no wiser as to what Clare was talking about than I was. Jenny looked unsettled, though, like the idea Clare might have something on her really bothered her. Even if she wasn't sure what it was.

I squished a pink marshmallow onto the top of a rice cracker, smearing it like a spread. It had been at the bottom of the bag, and had bits of peanut stuck to it. Probably bits of dirt and fluff too.

I wondered how long I would have to stay, for it not to look like I was leaving because of Clare. Not that I really cared what she thought, but I didn't want to give her the satisfaction. From Freya's expression, she was thinking the same thing.

It seemed to be another of this place's weird conventions, that ill feelings just got swept under the rug, rather than dealt with. I understood that, when it came to Amber and Jenny, but I couldn't for the life of me work out what Clare was holding over everyone else.

"So, ask me where I've been." Clare flashed her ridiculously shiny teeth at us.

I popped the cracker in my mouth so I wouldn't have to answer. Strangely, the combination of barbecue-flavoured rice cracker and raspberry marshmallow wasn't as bad as I would have thought. The bits of peanut caught in my throat, though, and I had to hold back a gag.

There was a silence, then Amber spoke. "Where have you been?" Her voice came out flat, lacking the enthusiasm Clare obviously wanted.

Clare was either oblivious to the atmosphere, or determined to ignore it. "Well, there's a little thing called the end of summer dance coming up."

Amber wrinkled her nose, unimpressed. "You'd think after running the thing for this many years, they wouldn't need an organising committee anymore."

Jenny nodded. "Yeah, I mean they're hardly reinventing the wheel."

Clare's cheeks flushed slightly, but her voice gave nothing away. "I may have been helping the guys out with their end-of-summer prank too, but of course I couldn't possibly say anything about that."

That got Jenny's attention. She sat up, leaning forward to cross Clare's eye line. "Seriously? You know what they're planning?"

Clare smirked, but didn't answer.

Jenny turned to Amber. "Oh god, I know it's going to be me," she wailed. "Come on, Clare, you've at least got to give me a hint." Jenny laughed, then she caught my eye. Her face fell, and she waved her hand at me like a sort of apology.

I shook my head. *It's okay*, I mouthed to her. I should have left when Clare arrived, rather than make them think they had to choose loyalties between us.

Jenny leaned back, her posture becoming awkward as she tried to feign disinterest.

Clare smiled, basking in the attention Jenny had given her a moment before.

"What's all this?" I asked. I tried to make myself sound interested for Jenny's sake. If I was honest, I was a little curious anyway.

Amber gave a mock-gasp. "Of course, Bailey, you're a newcomer."

"Every year–" Freya started, but Clare cut her off.

"You see, Bailey, it's tradition." Clare reached across to rest her hand on my knee. I fought the urge to flick her off, instead staring her straight in the eye. Clare faltered a little, then pulled her hand back and tossed her hair with it, as if that was what she'd meant to do all along.

"Every year there's the end-of-summer dance," she continued. "Then the next night two people get pranked. One boy, one girl."

"I just know it's going to be me this year," said Jenny. She shrugged as she said it. Another apology.

I couldn't tell whether she was horrified or excited by the idea. It seemed to be a mix of the two. I picked up another marshmallow, tearing it into quarters with my fingers. "What sort of prank?" I asked Clare, still keeping my voice light.

Clare gave me something that almost passed for a warm smile. "That's the fun, Bailey. You never know until it happens."

I frowned. That didn't sound like much fun to me. The way Clare said it made it sound more like a threat. The room went quiet again, and I could feel they were all waiting for me to ask another question. I wasn't sure there was anything else I wanted to know.

Amber cleared her throat. "That brings us to the very important point, of who we're going to pick."

"And what we're going to do," Jenny added. "Last year's jelly-in-the-underpants fell a bit flat."

"That was only because Chris realised before he sat down."

"What about Eddie?" Freya said. "Anyone know if he's been pranked in the last few years?"

Clare raised her eyebrows. "Interesting you'd pick him, Freya."

"What do you mean?" There was a blush creeping up Freya's neck. I got a sick feeling in my stomach, as I realised Clare was trying to start something.

Clare shrugged. "Well, just that I happened to be passing the equipment shed yesterday afternoon when you and Eddie were–"

"No way!" Jenny shrieked, grabbing Freya's shoulders. "You have to tell us everything."

Freya's face was bright red now. "It wasn't like that! We were just talking."

"Rumour has it he's going to ask you to the dance." Clare sat back with a self-satisfied smile as Jenny and Amber gushed. I frowned. Freya didn't seem to mind too much, but it was just the same old thing with Clare. Telling other people's secrets when it wasn't her place. If Freya had wanted to us to know, she would have told us herself.

I realised Clare was staring at me. She smiled when I met her eye, like we were sharing some kind of secret. I frowned and shook my head at her.

"Anyway," Amber said finally, "what are we going to do for our prank?"

I tore my focus away from Clare, though I could feel she didn't shift her gaze.

"Absolutely no jelly this year. It takes forever to set!"

I tried to feign interest in the discussion, but I wasn't really into it. After a while, I slipped out, saying I needed to check on Tilly.

"Don't you dare let on to any of the guys what we're planning, Bailey," Jenny called after me.

I gave an awkward salute. "Scout's honour."

• • • •

THE NEXT DAY, THE DANCE and the prank were all Jenny and Amber could talk about again. I was glad to be able to escape to the playground, though of course that set off a new round of whispers and sideways glances.

I kicked off my shoes, carrying them as I walked across the grass then dumping them next to me. The ground was surprisingly cold, holding moisture hostage despite the lack of rain. I remembered how my dad had always said that dogs had the right idea. Lying on a patch of grass was the best way to stay cool in summer. I could never work out whether it did actually make you cooler, or if it just felt so good you forgot the heat.

I didn't have plans to meet Adam at the playground, but even so I was more than a little happy to see him when he arrived not long after I did. I'd settled myself under a tree, at the far edge of the play area. Adam didn't see me straight away and I couldn't help but smile when I saw he was looking around for me.

"Hey, Adam!" Tilly waved to him from the jungle gym.

He grinned at her and waved back, then finally spotted me. His smile widened, turning into that big goofy one.

"Pretty good camouflage, Bailey," he called as he walked over.

"Well you know what they say about leopards," I called back. I felt my cheeks colour, as I realised that didn't make any sense.

Adam laughed anyway, and sat down next to me. We watched Tilly and Jack climbing up to the top of the jungle gym.

His arm was touching mine, the edge of his T-shirt sleeve brushing my shoulder, then his bare skin warm against mine. I didn't want to breathe, or I'd shift and make him think I was uncomfortable. I was, but I didn't want to pull away. It was so stupid; I don't think he'd even noticed.

Adam seemed relaxed. He smiled as he watched Jack running around.

"So, I gather I'm consorting with the enemy just by talking to you," I said after a bit.

"Huh?" Adam glanced at me.

I laughed. "This prank thing. Jenny practically had me swear on my parents' graves I wouldn't pass on any secrets. Do the guys take it that seriously too?"

"Oh, that." Adam settled back against the tree. "Yeah, it gets pretty competitive. They've roped Clare in to help them this year."

I shifted. "She said."

Adam and I hadn't talked about Clare since after I ran off from the pool. I wasn't sure if he knew how weird things still were, but he'd probably figured out she was at least part of the reason I was hanging out at the playground so much.

"So ..." Adam trailed off, and for a moment I thought that was all he was going to say. Then he took a breath. "Since you *can* swim, maybe I can teach you to surf after all." He stared at the playground as he said it, like he wasn't quite sure how I was going to react. Then he grinned. "Unless you don't think you can cope."

I opened my mouth in mock insult. "Excuse me? Competitive swimmer here."

"Yeah." He nodded, then tried to shake his head at the same time until he seemed to be lost in a rhythm all of his own. "I knew I recognised you on the first day, but I couldn't work out where from."

"Huh?"

"You don't remember?" Adam glanced over at me. "I used to compete, until I was thirteen. I remember you from Nationals."

I stared at him, then frowned. "When did you ...?" He knew I'd been lying the whole time. That's why he wasn't surprised when he caught me at the pool with Tilly, and why he didn't say anything. I covered my face. "Oh my god, that's so embarrassing."

Adam laughed. "It's all good."

I shook my head, then leaned it down on my knees. The sun had shifted in the time I'd been sitting there. I felt it creeping over my left arm, heating my skin millimetre by millimetre. "I'm sorry," I said to Adam through my hands. "You must have thought I was so weird for lying."

"It's okay. I didn't realise until I saw you coming back from the pool."

I wasn't sure why this was any different to before. Everyone who'd been at the pool when I fell in knew I'd been lying, and half of them probably thought I'd actually stabbed my parents. Somehow it felt worse that Adam had known all along, and had been waiting for me to recognise him and own up. I kept my hands over my face, but peered out from between my fingers. "Why didn't you say anything?" I shook my head. "God, I'm not even a good liar."

He shrugged. "I figured you just didn't want anyone to know how good you were, or something. Honestly, it's fine." Adam pulled my hands back from my face. He kept hold of my hands, his fingers warm against my palms. My fingers curled down instinctively, over the top of his.

He frowned as he stared at me. "You really don't remember me, though?"

I shook my head. "I never remember anything except the water." I blushed as I realised how pretentious that sounded. I wished I could reclaim the words out of the air before Adam heard them and lost all respect for me.

He just clucked his tongue. "God, you're one of those focused ones. That's why I stopped competing. Could never win against that."

He seemed to realise, suddenly, that he was still holding my hands. He let go and crossed his arms, tucking his hands away. I pushed my hair back off my face, feeling overly conscious of what I was doing. Things had gone awkward again, and I wasn't sure why. Adam settled back against the tree, and after a moment I joined him.

I watched him, staring at his profile until he caught my eye. I looked away quickly, like I had on the first day. He grinned then, I could tell, but I didn't look up. I suppose it was kind of bad that I didn't remember him, but people change a lot in a few years. I certainly didn't think I looked much like I did when I was thirteen. It was probably a fluke that Adam had been able to recognise me in the first place.

"We didn't meet at a McDonald's convention, or a vegetarian society meeting as well, did we?" I asked.

Adam didn't answer at first, then he shook his head. "I'm not sure." He gave an exaggerated sigh. "I'm always so focused at those McDonald's conventions; I never remember anything except the fish burgers."

I shoved his shoulder. "Shut up!"

He laughed and pushed me back. "*Shut up!*" he mimicked in a high voice.

"You're a dick."

"*You're a dick!*"

"Stop it!"

He opened his mouth, as if he were going to mimic that too, then he narrowed his eyes and held out his hand instead. "Truce?"

I eyed him, then took his hand. "Truce."

I picked at the grass. I'd been making a daisy chain for Tilly, but had abandoned it when Adam arrived. It was looped over my thigh, the petals starting to wilt. I picked it up and added to it, weaving in some of the little pink flowers that grew in the grass too.

Adam watched me. He picked a couple of daisies and handed them to me.

"Thanks."

He picked one of the pink flowers too, but didn't pass it to me. He twirled it between his fingers instead. "So, am I going to get any secrets out of you?" he asked.

I looked up at him. "Secrets?" My stomach tightened. His grin faltered as he looked at me, so I could tell my feelings were written all over my face.

"I meant the–"

I laughed as I figured it out about a second before he said it. "About the prank, you mean?" The tension in my stomach eased, as I realised he already knew my worst secrets anyway. I shrugged. "Name the right bribe, and we'll talk."

"Bribe?" Adam raised his eyebrows. "How about I torture it out of you instead?" Adam went to tickle me, but I caught his hand.

"You're out of luck. I'm the only truly non-ticklish person in the world."

"Seriously? I thought everyone was ticklish."

I nodded. "I know. Freak of nature." I wound the daisy chain around my neck, keeping it safe.

Adam sat back and shook his head. "That's so weird."

"I know. It's really weird." I stood up, brushing bits of grass from my clothes. "And totally not true." I took off running before he figured it out.

Eight

M UM USED TO WAKE me up at three a.m. every year
on my birthday. I was born at seven minutes past three,
and Mum said she wanted to celebrate the exact moment. Tilly
was born in the afternoon, so that was much easier.

Dad didn't like Mum waking me up so early. He thought
it would make me too tired during the day, but since my birthday always fell during the school holidays, Mum didn't think it
would matter.

Every year Mum would promise Dad she wasn't going to
do it, but we all knew she would. She'd wake me up, then we'd
blow out a candle and eat one of the cupcakes she'd made the
night before – half each. Then she'd always insist I brush my
teeth before going back to sleep.

I woke up at four thirty-two a.m. on my seventeenth birthday, and realised, for the first time in as long as I could remember, I had missed the moment I was born.

• • • •

I AVOIDED EVERYONE the next morning, spending far too
long in the shower in lieu of going for a swim. I clenched my
jaw tight every time thoughts of cupcakes and birthday candles
tried to creep in, until the side of my face started to hurt.

Adam didn't come up to the kids' area to see Jack, and I was
annoyed to find I was disappointed. We hadn't made any plans
to meet, so I had no right to be, really. It was probably better
he didn't come up anyway. I was feeling maudlin, and he'd seen
me cry enough this week as it was.

I knew I ought to go visit Gran. Tilly was too little to know what the date was, let alone remember it was my birthday, but Gran would. I didn't want to face it, though. It was too weird to celebrate without Mum and Dad.

I slipped away just before lunch, letting the staff take Tilly down to the dining hall. Anne smiled when I did that, but I could only manage a sort of mouth shrug in return.

I thought about going back to the cabins, spending the day avoiding people and pretending to sleep. The little growl in my stomach told me I wouldn't get away with that for long. I held off for a while anyway, hoping most people would have finished their lunch and left by the time I got around to it.

Jenny was sitting outside the dining hall when I finally went down. She scratched at some dry skin on her arm, fully absorbed in making the white flakes detach themselves and scatter. I watched them too. It would be pretty if you didn't know it was dead skin.

Jenny looked up when my shadow fell over her. "There you are!" She reached out for my hand. I hesitated, then took hers and braced myself as she hauled herself to her feet.

"Were you waiting for me?" I asked.

"We all are."

My stomach twisted as she said that. Thoughts of fleeing filled my head, but she still had my hand captured in hers. "Why?"

"Look who I found," Jenny yelled, cutting me off.

I stumbled on the doorstop, but Jenny gripped my hand, steadying me. She didn't respond to my question, but the answer was pretty obvious anyway.

Adam turned around in his seat. Tilly and Jack were sitting on either side of him, but they didn't look up. There was a cake in the middle of the table, and their eyes were glued to it.

"Finally!" Amber got up from the table to give me a hug. "We thought you were never going to show up."

"I went for a walk," I said into Amber's shoulder.

Clare stepped forward, nudging Amber away. "Happy birthday," she said.

I froze as she put her arms around me. She patted my back gently, like she wasn't quite sure what to do with her hands. I forced myself to hug her back, in the hope that it would make her let go quicker. Her chin was digging into my shoulder, and her hair smelt like a mixture of toothpaste and bubblegum shampoo.

Jenny cleared her throat, and Clare finally let go. I met her eye for a second, then she stepped back, crossing her arms over her chest and staring in the other direction. She looked like she was in pain, or really cold perhaps. I frowned. Was wishing me a happy birthday really that much of a source of stress for her?

"Surprise!" Jenny yelled. She waggled her fingers, making jazz hands. I blinked, tearing my gaze away from Clare, then started laughing. The timing of that made it more confusing than surprising.

"How did you know?" I asked.

Amber tussled Tilly's hair. "Your little sister can't keep a secret to save herself."

Tilly squirmed away from Amber, hiding her face in my stomach. I picked her up and hugged her. "Thank you, bub." I buried my face in her hair for a moment.

On my last birthday, Mum had forced me to give Tilly a hug when she gave me the birthday card she'd made for me. But Tilly had run off screaming that I had boy germs all over me from kissing David, and I couldn't be bothered chasing her. Mum was upset about that, I think.

I squeezed Tilly tighter. It was funny to think that Mum used to have to make us hug. I looked up as Adam stood.

"You'd better cut the cake," he said. He handed me a knife and nodded towards Jack. "I can't hold this one off for much longer."

I felt a little squirm inside me as I realised I'd been wondering if he was going to hug me too. I suppose he couldn't have, really, with me holding Tilly, but I got the feeling he wouldn't have anyway. I busied myself with cutting the cake, so he wouldn't see I was blushing.

Tilly shifted so I could reach the table, but Jack stayed right where he was. I could see what Adam meant. There were little fingerprints around the base of the cake, where Jack had stolen icing.

There were no birthday candles, which I was glad about. I cut the cake one-handed, balancing Tilly against my hip. I wanted to hide my face too, as everyone clapped and sang happy birthday.

"Sit down," Amber said when they'd finished. "We'll get you some lunch."

There were dirty plates on the table, so they must have given up waiting for me and eaten already. No wonder Adam had been having trouble holding Tilly and Jack back from the cake.

Amber and Jenny dragged Clare off with them. She seemed reluctant to go. Perhaps she didn't trust me alone with Adam, even when we had two kids climbing all over us. I wanted to ask her why she was even here. Surely she hadn't been clamouring to celebrate my birth?

"So what did you wish for?" Adam asked.

"Huh?"

He nodded towards the cake. "The knife came out clean. You should get your wish." He grinned.

I shook my head. "Can't tell you that. Won't come true."

The truth was I hadn't actually made a wish. My mind always went blank with those things, and I could never think of anything that seemed worth the ritual. But that sounded silly. I didn't want to admit to being so boring I couldn't think of a single wish.

I glanced over at the buffet. Clare's method of helping appeared to be to stand next to Amber and Jenny while they got the food. I shook my head. At least she was trying, I guess.

"Put that back!"

Adam's voice made me jump. I thought he was talking to me, then I saw Jack sneaking another slice of cake onto his plate. He stepped back from the table with the cake still in his hands. If he was anything like Tilly, he'd keep taking little steps backwards until he was out of grabbing range, then make a run for it.

"Michael would let me have more." Jack's voice was sulky.

I pressed my hand against my mouth to stop myself laughing at his pouty-face.

Adam shook his head. "No, he wouldn't. Put it back."

Jack hesitated, then dumped the second slice of cake back onto the plate. It toppled over, the end of the wedge breaking off into a little detached triangle.

Jack glared at me, as if it were my fault he wasn't getting a second piece. I shrugged – my default answer to all of Tilly's tantrums. Jack didn't like it any more than Tilly did. He turned his back on me and stomped off to the kids' table. After a second, Tilly slid off my lap to follow him.

"Who's Michael?" I asked Adam.

Adam didn't answer at first. He stared at his fork, twisting it back and forth between his fingers. "Our older brother," he said eventually. He put the fork down on his plate, letting it clatter.

"I thought it was just you and Jack." As soon as I said it, I got a horrible feeling that Michael was dead. My face heated up, thinking how insensitive that must have sounded.

But Adam shook his head. "Nope, there are three of us."

I let out a breath. His lips made a popping noise on the "nope", like there was some anger attached to it. He wasn't looking at me, but staring at the fork again. Glaring at it, actually.

"Adam ..." I trailed off, not sure what I was going to say next. He didn't seem to hear me, anyway. I grabbed the fork, making him look at me.

He looked surprised, then after a second he grinned. "Jack likes to play us off one another. Just be glad there's only the two of you, or Tilly would be trying it too."

I nodded slowly. "Yeah." I wasn't quite sure what had just happened, but it seemed Michael was a no-go topic. I forced a smile. "Tilly does her best with me and Gran, so you're probably right."

Adam shook his head. "When we were their age, we respected our elders."

I rolled my eyes. "Sure. And we walked to school in two metres of snow." I half stood up, brushing Tilly's cake crumbs from my legs.

"Burning heat." Adam tilted his head towards the window. "Walked eleven kilometres in burning heat. It's more believable."

I shook my head. "Sure. 'Believable.'"

Adam made a dismissive motion with his hand. "What would you know? You're only seventeen."

I laughed. "Seventeen, as opposed to?"

"Seventeen and ..." he counted on his fingers, "five months. I've got practically a lifetime of experience on you."

I shook my head and laughed. "Whatever, Adam."

Amber and Jenny slid into the seats either side of me. Clare hovered for a moment, then sat down next to Adam. He twisted his shoulder, as if he was going to turn away from her, then seemed to catch himself. He leaned back in the chair instead. His foot hit my shin as he stretched his legs out and I drew my feet up underneath me. If this was Adam's attempt at looking relaxed, it wasn't working.

I realised I was still holding his fork captive. I set it down on the table, so we could all have a go at staring at it instead of looking at each other.

"Here we go." Amber put a plate in front of me. She'd arranged the salad into a smiley face. "All vege approved, at Adam's insistence."

"God, you're not still on that are you?" Clare rolled her eyes. "You've got to stop trying to convert people, Adam."

I shook my head. "He didn't–"

"Bailey was vegetarian long before she met me, Clare." There was more anger in Adam's tone than was warranted by the topic. He picked up the fork and started twisting it between his fingers again.

Clare gave me a tight-lipped smile. "Well, that's nice then, isn't it?"

I felt an intense need to giggle at her puckered-up face. The word "nice" had never sounded so menacing before.

"Thanks," I said to Amber. I gestured towards the food to make it clear what I was talking about.

It was obviously an argument Clare and Adam had had many times. I'd had hard-core meat eaters get pissy about the vegetarian thing before, but Clare made it feel like she might actually turn cannibal to prove her point.

I picked up my own fork, but it felt weird to eat when everyone else had already finished. "You guys have some cake," I said.

Jenny let out a breath. "Man, I thought you were never going to offer."

I laughed as she dished out massive pieces for her and Amber.

Adam shook his head. "You guys are worse than Jack."

It was a fabulous-looking cake. There were two layers, with another layer of icing in the middle. That had always been my favourite part of the cake. If I'd been young enough to get away with it, I'd have stuck my fingers in the icing, just like Jack had.

"Good, you guys are still here!"

I looked up as Freya came rushing in the door.

She let out breath, turning her words into a sigh. "Sorry I'm late." She took off her glasses, holding them out so we could see. "Damned things broke. Eddie fixed them for me."

The arm of Freya's glasses had been reattached with a paper clip. Eddie hadn't broken the ends off, so they stuck out like a mangled butterfly and there was a red mark on her temple where they'd been digging into the side of her face. It seemed glasses weren't actually any more convenient than the contacts had been.

Amber scrunched up her nose. "Number eight wire would work better."

Freya rolled her eyes. "And do you have any number eight wire?"

Amber shrugged. "Not on me."

"Didn't think so." Freya grinned at me. "Anyway, happy birthday, Bailey."

Freya sat down next to Clare. She knocked the table, and Clare's coffee toppled over, spilling out across the table top and onto Clare's lap. I started to laugh, but Clare's face went hard. She grabbed Adam's juice, dumping the contents over Freya.

I covered my mouth; Amber's and Jenny's hands flew to their faces too.

"Clare!" Adam grabbed the glass from her, but it was already empty.

It was cranberry juice, and Freya's shorts were white. It spread in a big pink stain, until it looked like her clothes had been tie-dyed. I stared at the paper cup Clare's coffee had been in. It rolled across the table in a tilted spiral.

I didn't look up at Clare. She seemed startled, though. I could tell she and Adam were staring at each other, then he shifted, actually turning away this time.

"Sorry," Clare mumbled to Freya. "I don't know why I did that."

Freya shook her head. "You're a bitch, that's why you did it." She stood up, shaking the excess liquid onto the floor.

There was a moment where I thought maybe I'd imagined Freya saying that. She didn't shout it or anything, just said it quietly, like a statement of fact.

Clare stared at the table in front of her. I didn't dare move, in case I caught her attention and got my own beverage shower. The coffee spill was still spreading, and in a second it would be dripping off our side of the table, over me, Jenny and Amber.

"We should clean that up." Adam gestured towards the coffee. He glanced at Freya and cleared his throat, like he was going to say something to her, but then walked off towards the kitchen instead. I had a feeling he wouldn't be coming back anytime soon. Getting caught in the middle of other people's arguments was never fun, and his and Clare's history was hardly going to make that better.

Clare stood up, bashing the table in the process. I grabbed my water, pulling it out of her reach. The coffee had barely touched her. There was a smattering of brown spots over her thighs, but it was nothing like the amount of juice over Freya.

Clare made a little sound; the beginning of a sob.

Freya sighed. "Clare ..."

"Just shut up!" Clare pushed past Freya, and ran outside.

I stared at the salad in front of me. It seemed rude to continue eating, but I was still really hungry.

Freya shrugged. "It could be worse," she said. "If it was apple juice, I'd look like I'd wet myself."

I cracked up, laying my head down on the table as I laughed. I could feel Jenny doing the same. She leaned against me, practically crying she was laughing so hard.

"I'm sorry," I said. "It's just ... oh my god!"

Freya shook her head. "She's a total nut job." She was laughing too, though.

Amber was the only one who wasn't. She ran her finger around the rim of her glass of water, like she was trying to coax a tune out of it.

Jenny sighed. "Babe–" she started, but Amber raised her glass, cutting her off.

"A toast," she said and looked at me. "To birthdays ... and total nut jobs." She threw the water over herself.

It took me a second too long to realise what was happening. Jenny grabbed her juice and threw it over me.

I wiped a bit of orange pulp from my cheek. "No way." I shook my head. Jenny grinned at me. I picked up my glass, and she ran for it.

• • • •

"HEY, BAILEY." ADAM caught up with me later, as I was walking back to the cabins. I turned towards his voice.

"Whoa, what happened?" Adam frowned as I turned around. I glanced at the splash pattern of water and juice down the front of my top.

I shook my head. "Nothing. Amber started a 'water fight' after you left." I blushed at how childish that sounded.

Adam looked confused, but he seemed relieved as well. I realised he'd probably thought Clare had doused me, and no matter how childish a water fight was it was better than that.

Adam had a dab of icing on his cheek, left over from the cake at lunch. He grinned. "Happy birthday," he said.

"Thanks."

"I wasn't sure if that was okay ... at lunch." He frowned for a moment, staring at the ground.

A reverse leopard-print of sunlight fell through the leaves above us onto our skin. I looked up at Adam. Was he talking about Clare? No, it wasn't okay that she'd had a tantrum and chucked juice everywhere. But that didn't mean Adam needed to apologise for her. I opened my mouth to say as much, but he continued before I could.

"Tilly told me it was your birthday, but since you hadn't said anything ..."

"Oh, that." I shook my head. "It was fine." I smiled. "Nice, actually. I didn't think Tilly would remember."

Adam's face relaxed, turning his frown from the deep one into the softer, regular one. His gaze drifted away from me. I leaned back against a tree, letting the bark scratch the spot between my shoulder blades.

"I told them no cupcakes," Adam said quietly.

"Huh?" I felt myself go cold. I stared at him, but he wasn't looking at me.

"Tilly said your mum always made cupcakes. I figured ..." He didn't finish that, perhaps realising any anguish he'd saved me by avoiding the cupcakes would be lost if we talked about it.

I swallowed. "Thank you," I said. "That's incredibly ... perceptive ... of you." I wasn't sure if that was the right word. It was half masked by the crack in my voice, anyway. I blinked, forcing back the tears I could feel building up.

"Yeah, well."

I could tell there was a story there. A reason he knew what would upset me on my first birthday without my parents. He wasn't going to say it right now, though, and it wasn't my place to ask.

I wondered if this would be me in a few years, comforting someone else who'd just lost a parent, and having the burden of knowing what was and wasn't going to be painful.

Adam looked up at me. "I was wondering if you wanted to go to the dance with me? Just as friends, I mean."

My stomach did a little flip-flop as he said that, rising up then sinking down fast as he added the "just friends". As platonic as you can get.

I nodded. "Yeah, that'd be good." My answer didn't sound particularly enthusiastic. I was still pushing the need to cry back down inside me. Hopefully he would understand that, though.

"Cool." There was a pause, and then he grinned. "I'd say I'd pick you up, but–"

"Not a rule-breaker, I know." I smiled. "I'll meet you there."

I swung my arms, not really knowing what to do with myself. I brushed my hands down my front again, as if I might have missed some crumbs. Finally I looked up at him again. "Well, I'd better ..." I gestured down the path, as if there was something really important I had to do back at the cabins.

"Yeah, me too." Adam nodded. "See you later, Bailey."

I turned away, then called back over my shoulder. "Hey, Adam?"

"Yeah?"

I glanced back at him. "You have icing on your cheek." I grinned at him as he wiped it off.

Nine

I USED TO FEEL LIKE MUM loved Tilly more than me. Tilly liked dressing up. She liked all the girly things that just made me feel awkward and self-conscious. When I got home from school each day, I'd hear them laughing in Mum's room as they played with Mum's makeup, or did each other's hair. I took to going to the pool straight after school so I wouldn't feel like I was missing out on something.

After Mum died, I realised maybe it was the other way around. Maybe it wasn't Mum who loved Tilly more than she did me. Maybe it was Tilly who loved Mum more than I ever could.

• • • •

THE AFTERNOON BEFORE the dance, Amber and Jenny appeared with a million outfits to try on. Our cabin had a bigger mirror, so they were in and out until I said they could just stay to try stuff on.

It was funny to watch. They both had to try each dress, though with Amber being a good twenty centimetres taller, everything that fit her was too long on Jenny, and all Jenny's clothes were too small for Amber. It didn't stop them trying, though. Freya's bed was covered in layers of clothing as they discarded outfit after outfit.

"What are you wearing, Bailey?" Jenny asked, as she pulled off yet another dress that didn't fit.

I shrugged. "Not sure. How formal is this thing?" Most of what I'd packed was pretty casual – basically anything that wouldn't be ruined by over-exposure to chlorine, as I'd figured I'd be spending a good amount of time at the pool. Sometimes it seemed like my clothes worked out just as hard as I did, growing thinner and thinner as the chemicals broke down the threads.

"So-so." Amber started poking through my bag, pulling out items of clothing.

"Hey!" I got up to stop her.

She sighed, dramatically. "That lot is a disaster, Bailey. Did you even bring any makeup?"

I shook my head. Back home, I was in the water so much I didn't bother, except on special occasions, and I hadn't figured this would be that kind of place.

Amber went back to sifting through her and Jenny's pile of clothing. She pulled out a pale-pink, floaty dress. "Try this on." She held it out to me, but Jenny snatched it out of her hand.

"No way, that will totally wash her out." She rummaged through the pile of clothes herself, pulling out a dark-purple dress instead. "Try this one."

"It's okay, you guys don't have to–"

"Are you kidding? This is Jenny's dream come true."

Jenny nodded. "I'm an only child. Never got to dress up a little sister." She covered her mouth, feigning holding back tears. "Even a little brother would have done, if he could have stood the makeup."

I laughed. "All right, fine."

I ducked into the bathroom to change. I knew they'd already seen them, but I couldn't get over feeling weird about exposing the scars in front of other people. It was like a new level of nakedness. Like the wound was still open, spilling my insides out in front of them. I couldn't even look down, when I got changed alone, without feeling obscene.

The purple dress was tighter than anything I wore normally. I had to breathe in, and practically dislocate my elbows just to get into it.

But Jenny clapped her hands as I came back into the cabin. "Ooo, yes!"

I laughed as I saw my reflection. "No way."

Jenny's face fell into a pout. "Why not? The colour's perfect on you."

I pulled at the front of the dress. It was puckering up, like it objected to the situation as much as I did. "It's too small and way too low cut. I'll fall out if I'm not careful."

"Oh come on, a little cleavage is fine."

I shook my head. It was too much. Going from beachwear to night club in one bound was more than my confidence could take.

Amber nodded. "She's right, Babe. There's cleavage, and then there's," Amber gestured towards me, "ridiculous."

I cracked up, and Jenny reluctantly nodded. "All right, if you two are going to be prudes!" She picked up a turquoise dress. "Amber, can she try this on?"

Amber nodded. "Of course, try anything you like. That one doesn't fit me anyway, so you're welcome to it."

I ducked out into the bathroom again, to try it on. I could tell even without seeing my reflection that this was a better fit. I could actually take a deep breath for a start. The colour reminded me of something, too. A dress of Mum's, or a scarf maybe. Whatever it was, it was probably long gone by now; sold in a secondhand shop after the house was packed up.

Freya was hovering in the doorway when I came back into the cabin.

"Sorry, hun, they've taken over your bed," I said to her.

She shrugged. "It's okay." She plonked herself down on my bed, and watched while Jenny fussed over my outfit. I avoided looking in the mirror. I liked this dress, but I was afraid I wouldn't once I added my own image into the mix.

"What are you wearing, Freya?" Amber asked her.

Freya made a face. "Not sure if I'm going to go."

"Why not?" Jenny stopped what she was doing to stare at Freya. "I thought you were going with Eddie?"

Freya shrugged. She took her glasses off, dumping them on the floor beside the bed, then rolled over onto her stomach. I picked up the glasses. I knew I'd never forgive myself if I broke them, and if they were left on the floor, the potential of that happening was pretty high. The insides of the lenses were flecked with white dots. Salt. Just like my sunglasses always were, after I tried to hide behind them while crying.

I sat down on the bed, next to Freya. Comforting people wasn't my strong suit. I rested my hand on her shoulder, hoping it didn't seem as awkward to her as it felt to me. "Eddie didn't ask you?" I said.

Freya shook her head. Amber and Jenny went quiet. I could tell they had the same thoughts as me running through their heads. There was the option of faking optimism – telling Freya he was probably just waiting for the right moment, and that she shouldn't get too upset. Or we could be honest with her, and say if he hadn't asked her by now he probably wasn't going to.

Jenny forced a laugh. "You know how disorganised guys are," she said. "He's probably forgotten the dance is tomorrow, and just–"

"He's going with Clare." Freya looked back over her shoulder at Jenny.

"With Clare?" I shook my head. "Why?" I didn't really expect an answer to that question, but I couldn't believe it. Eddie had seemed so keen on Freya. Why on earth would he want to go with someone like Clare instead? For that matter, why did Clare want to go with him?

Freya shrugged. "Don't know. Josh told me about it."

Amber frowned. "No way. Clare said he was going to ask you. She wouldn't have ..."

Jenny met my eye, and scrunched up her nose as Amber trailed off. Freya's shoulder was heating up under my touch, making my palm sticky and uncomfortable. I pulled my hand back, folding it in my lap. By now it had gone from being a supportive gesture to bordering on creepy, anyway.

Jenny moved over to Amber, leaning against her and rubbing her back. Amber seemed almost more upset than Freya was. I wondered if she'd ever be able to let go of her idea of Clare, or if she'd always be waiting for her to go back to being nice. If she ever had genuinely been nice, that was.

It was kind of soothing to watch the way Jenny reacted to Amber. They seemed so in sync, like they always knew what the other needed without having to say it. I glanced at Freya.

"Boys are dumb," I said. It's what my best friend had always said to me when I had a fight with David, and it had always made me laugh. In a weird way it made me laugh even more to think of her saying it about him now.

Freya frowned. For a moment I thought I'd made things worse, but then she nodded. "Super dumb."

"Clare's dumb too," Amber added.

Jenny raised her eyebrows at me, but didn't say anything.

Freya almost cracked a smile, then she rubbed her eyes. "She's not dumb," she said. She added something else under her breath, probably keeping her voice low for Amber's benefit. I didn't quite catch it, but I think "she's a spiteful cow" was probably the gist.

I wondered if Clare had told Eddie that Freya didn't want to go with him, so he wouldn't bother asking. It seemed like her style – make crap up just to see what would happen. A horrible thought occurred to me. Maybe he'd never been going to ask her in the first place, and Clare had made *that* up to be mean.

I shook my head. It didn't really matter how she'd done it; Clare had managed to thoroughly drive a wedge through that relationship. I wondered what possible pleasure she could get from that.

"Well, don't worry, Cinderella, you shall go to the ball." Jenny mimed donking Freya on the head with a magic wand. "We'll go as a group; you won't even notice what's-his-face isn't with you."

"Yeah, it's just a pity Bailey's going with a dumb boy." Amber grinned at me.

I shrugged. "We're just going as friends. He can be an honorary girl for the night." I thought of suggesting Jenny find Adam a dress for the night, but then I worried she might take me seriously. I stood up from the bed, letting the fabric of the turquoise dress swish around my legs. "Come on," I said to

Freya. "Be Jenny's honorary sister for a bit, and let her dress you up."

"Ooo, yes, I have the perfect dress for you, Freya."

Freya made a face but I pulled her arm, hauling her off the bed.

"Just go with it." I nodded towards the pile of dresses, and grinned at Freya. "It's easier than resisting."

I ducked back out to the bathroom to change, as Jenny started fussing over Freya's clothes. Much as she was pretending to hate it, I caught a glimpse of a smile on Freya's face as I left.

• • • •

I HAD ANOTHER NIGHTMARE that night. It didn't matter how many times it happened, I still panicked every time I woke suddenly in the middle of the night. It wasn't my usual nightmare, though. There were no kitchens, and no sign of blood. Just high heels and staircases with Clare waiting to push me down them. Now that I was awake, it was almost more funny than scary.

I didn't move for a moment, letting my heart rate slow, in the hope that I'd be able to drop back to sleep without too much stress. It was wishful thinking. Tilly's elbow was pressing into my bladder, and the need to go to the bathroom had probably disturbed my sleep more than the nightmare itself.

I slid my arm around Tilly's shoulder, rolling her onto her side without waking her. I'd gotten pretty good at that lately. She'd always been a heavy sleeper, but after Mum and Dad died the slightest hint of noise would have her wide awake in seconds. I'd had to develop a whole series of tricks to be able to get out of bed. It was just a pity it wasn't a talent that translated into anything much else.

Someone flushed the toilet as I walked into the bathroom. I thought of running for the second stall so I could shut the door before they opened theirs, and we wouldn't have to see each other. I never got where the idea that women can't go to the bathroom alone came from. As far as I'm concerned, there's something acutely awkward about talking to another person when you're just about to pee.

The stall door opened before I made up my mind, and Clare came out. I stared at her for a moment, then scuttled for the toilet stall. She smirked as I did.

"Not going to say hello, Bailey? That's not very nice."

I shut the door behind me, hoping she'd get the message and go away. I heard the taps running as she washed her hands.

"That's your thing, though, isn't it? Nice as pie when there are other people around, but then it's all skulking around and lying when you're by yourself."

I sat down on the toilet seat. I wondered if Clare actually thought that made sense, or if she was just saying whatever came into her head in the hope that some of it would upset me. It was making it difficult to pee; I had to admit that much.

"Do Amber and Jenny know how two-faced you are? Do you think they'd want to hang around with you if they did?" Clare gave a little laugh. "Do you think Adam would?"

So that's what this was about. Adam. She must have heard we were going to the dance together. I thought of the heart on the wall, with their names in it. It wouldn't matter what I said to defend myself, she'd still consider herself scorned.

I stood up, retying my pyjama shorts. My feet were cold, bare against the chill of the tiles. I wanted to get out of there and go back to bed, but I didn't want to have to walk past Clare.

What the hell was she doing, anyway? It sounded like she was brushing her teeth. It wouldn't have surprised me if she was hanging around just to make me uncomfortable. I came out of the stall, but didn't look up at her.

Clare *had* been cleaning her teeth. The entire contents of her sponge bag were laid out over the washbasin, and now she was brushing her hair.

I pumped soap onto my hands. The sink wasn't very clean. There were flecks of toothpaste, and goodness knows what else all over the basin. I couldn't tell whether they were just from Clare, or from several days' worth of people, and it made me feel dirty just to touch the taps.

"You know, Bailey, what I really worry about is your sister."

I froze as Clare said that. She saw my reaction and kept going, knowing she'd hit her mark.

"With your parents gone, you're her only influence. Is she going to grow up to be a little liar, just like you?"

My eyes blurred as I stared at the water flowing over my hands. Clare twisted in front of the mirror and carried on brushing her hair. She must have known she'd hurt me with that last comment, but she wasn't even the slightest bit ashamed. Hell, she actually seemed pleased with herself.

I looked up, meeting her eye in the mirror. "We're all going to get ready together tomorrow," I said. "I wondered if you wanted to join us."

Clare frowned. She opened her mouth to answer, but I cut her off.

"Oh, no, that's right. You're probably keeping your distance since you decided to ask Eddie, when you knew he was planning to go with Freya. You're pretty good at screwing over your friends, aren't you, Clare?"

That was mean, and I knew it. My thoughts were raging, though; fighting between the part of me that hated Clare and wanted to make her cry, and the other part that knew that was cruel, no matter what she'd done.

Clare rolled her eyes. I hadn't figured out what I wanted to say next. I knew it had to be me who said it, though, since everyone else was so much under her thumb.

"That was really mean," I said. Even to me it sounded pathetic. Clare was willing to cross lines to hurt people, but I wasn't.

Clare sighed and stared at me. She tapped her hairbrush against the palm of her hand. She was a mess. Her hair looked like it was forming dreads as we spoke, and there were food stains down the front of her pyjamas. At least, they looked like food stains. There was a nasty smell in the room. Sickly sweet, like bile. I looked down at Clare's sponge bag, her toothbrush just used.

"Anything else?" Clare asked.

I shook my head, losing my resolve. "No. That's all I wanted to say."

We stared at each other for a moment, then I turned away. I hesitated when I got to the doorway, and looked back towards Clare. She was watching me leave.

"What are you doing in here, anyway?" I asked. "This isn't your bathroom."

Clare shrugged, like it was a stupid question. It wasn't, though. It was the middle of the night. There couldn't possibly be a shortage of space in her bathroom, so what was she doing in ours?

I nodded towards the toilet stall. "Did you just throw up?" I asked.

Clare went very still. She had her head tilted forward, her hair blocking her face from view. I couldn't see her expression, but that stillness was enough for me to know I was right.

"That's more your style, isn't it, Bailey?" she said eventually. Her voice came out flat and cold, not even pretending to laugh it off. "Doing things in secret, like a little drama queen." She shook her head.

I hesitated, then stepped back into the room. It was easier looking at her in the mirror, rather than meeting her eye directly. I stood behind her, waiting.

She rummaged around in her sponge bag, trying to look busy.

"Do you do it often?" I asked. I didn't know enough to be sure whether that mattered. Was making yourself sick once just a moment of bad decision, and any more than that an eating disorder? Either way, I wasn't sure I had the emotional capacity to want to help her.

Clare rolled her eyes. "Just go away, Bailey."

I dropped my gaze, staring at my feet. They'd adjusted to the chill of the tiles now, but under the glare of the fluorescent lights my skin looked mauve. I remembered Adam's comment about Clare: *She's not a bad person; she just does stupid things.*

I wondered if she knew that's how he felt, or if she thought he hated her for all her screw ups.

"No-one asked you to the dance, did they?" I said. "That's why you asked Eddie."

She went still again, but then she smirked and raised her eyebrows. I held her eye, waiting. The smirk started to falter.

"I'm sorry," I said. I tried to fill my voice with compassion, but it was hard to feel anything other than irritation towards Clare. "That sucks." I paused, then let myself add what I was really thinking. "But so did doing that to Freya."

Clare shook her head and scoffed. "So sanctimonious, Bailey." The smile dropped from her face, and she swallowed hard. "Exactly how is it any different to you going with Adam?"

There were a lot of answers I could have given. It was different because I'd tried to make it right with her and Adam, and she'd thrown it back in my face. It was different because he'd asked me, not the other way around. It was different because we were only going as friends and I wasn't going with him just to be cruel.

Mostly it was different because if she'd asked him, I'm sure he would have gone with her instead of me.

I walked away without saying any of them.

Ten

THE FIRST TIME I went out with David, Tilly had wanted to come with me. Nothing I said could convince her she couldn't. Not that I tried very hard. I think I just told her no, without giving her any reason.

Mum told me it would be fine, to just go out and enjoy myself and not worry about what Tilly was doing. I did. I went out and didn't think about her once all night.

She was asleep when I got home, but she'd had a tantrum while I'd been out. I could tell by the red patches on her cheeks, and the way her breath wheezed, thick with mucus.

Mum never mentioned it. It could have been a tantrum about something else. Some perceived slight on Mum's part, like not letting her have ice-cream instead of dinner. I didn't ask, though. I was scared Mum would tell me it was a tantrum because of me, and I didn't want to know.

• • • •

I FALTERED OUTSIDE the dining hall – or dance hall, as it now was – but I was swept along by Jenny and Amber. After trying on a million different outfits at Jenny's insistence, I'd finally ended up back in the turquoise dress, and a pair of Amber's heels. At the last minute, I'd added a pair of peacock feather earrings and a silver bracelet that had been hiding in my sponge bag. Jenny gushed over them, saying the colours were perfect. I didn't tell her they were my mother's; that would have put a dampener on things. I felt stronger once I put them on, though, like my mum was with me.

Amber did my makeup for me, then practically sat on Freya, forcing her to have hers done too. Freya still wasn't that keen to go. I think she was planning on backing out at the last minute, but Amber and Jenny kept up such a momentum getting us all ready that I think even she began to enjoy it.

Inside the hall, the decorations were far more impressive than I'd been expecting. The walls were covered in little silver petals, and there were strings of purple fairy lights strung across the ceiling. I touched one of the petals, and laughed. They were made of tinfoil, but combined with the lights they made everything shimmer and sparkle.

I saw Adam, standing in the far corner. He was wearing a white shirt, and had his back to me. His shirt seemed to shimmer silver and purple too.

He turned around as I walked over, and his face morphed into that goofy grin. "Bailey," he said.

I felt silly and shy, suddenly. No better than Tilly playing dress ups in Mum's clothes.

"You look ..." He took my hand and smiled. "Gorgeous."

People moved to the dance floor as music started up. The hall was actually a lot bigger than I'd thought, once all the tables were folded away. Even with everyone dancing, there was still heaps of room to move around.

Adam tilted his head towards the dance floor. "Do you want to ...?"

I shook my head, shy again. "I'm not much of a dancer."

Adam let out a breath and grinned. "Me neither."

We went to sit down instead, and Adam got me some juice. I took a sip then spat it back into the cup as I tasted it. I coughed and set the cup down next to my feet.

"That's half alcohol," I said.

Adam laughed. He kept hold of his cup, but drank slowly.

I shifted my cup, moving it away from my foot so I wouldn't knock it over, finally sliding it right under the chair. Amber's dress would be ruined by flying juice, and I didn't have much trust in my ability to keep my limbs out of range. Adam watched me, but didn't comment. Perhaps he understood the anxiety involved in balancing a disposable cup on the ground and praying for it not to tip.

"So, when are we going surfing?" he asked. "Auckland's not that far from Paihia, but I'll have to plan it around all those McDonald's conventions." He grinned.

I shook my head. "You're not going to let that go, are you?"

"Nope."

I shrugged. I hadn't been to the beach since I'd moved to Gran's. I wasn't as strong in the surf as I was in a pool, but water was water and I'd always loved it. "I have to warn you," I said, "my balance is surprisingly bad."

I looked down at my feet, in Amber's ridiculously high heels. If I made it through the night without falling over, it would be a miracle.

Adam glanced down. "Not trying to surf in heels would be my first tip."

I shook my head and tried not to laugh. "Shut up."

"I'm going to get a complex if you keep telling me to shut up, Bailey." Adam grinned.

I rolled my eyes. "You won't let me apologise; you won't let me tell you to shut up …"

Adam didn't answer. I looked up, following his eye line, but I already knew what I was going to see. Clare and Eddie stood in the doorway, the silver petals framing them, like the sunlight had framed Clare on the first day. She looked gorgeous in a white dress, her shiny hair flowing out around her, no sign of any dreads now. Eddie looked uncomfortable as she dragged him along by the hand.

I looked back at Adam. His face was unreadable – too many emotions, fighting each other, to form an expression. He glanced at me, and his face flitted through another series of emotions, all of them too fast for me to catch.

I think my face was probably doing the same.

"Do you want to go sit outside?" he asked me finally.

I nodded. "Sure."

Adam relaxed again, as we sat down on the edge of the deck outside the hall. The mood was gone, though. It was too hard to be light and jokey when I knew his mind was back inside with Clare.

"You still like her, don't you?" I regretted it as soon as it was out of my mouth. There was nothing I could do about it, though. Just wait.

Adam stared at me, and his frown was definitely a frown. In the dark his eyes seemed black, like his pupils had swollen to flood over the iris. He held my eye, then looked away and cleared his throat. I dropped my gaze.

The wood on the deck was splitting around the nails. I picked at it, pulling splinters free. I almost wished one of them would stab into my thumb, to give me something else to focus on.

Adam sculled his drink and got up. "I'm going to get another drink," he said. He hesitated, like he was going to say something else, but then he walked back inside without looking at me.

"That was stupid, Bailey," I said to myself.

I leaned back on my elbows and stretched my legs out in front of me. Amber's heels had little silver rhinestones set in them, which glinted against the light. I closed one eye, then the other, making the light bounce back and forth.

Adam didn't come out again for ages, and after a while I started to wonder if he wasn't going to. It wouldn't have surprised me. *I* wanted to run away from me right now.

Finally he appeared with two cups. He held one out to me. "Found some that wasn't spiked."

"Thanks." I went to take it from him, but he pulled it back.

"Wait." He frowned and weighed the cups up in his hands.

"Forgotten which is which?"

He looked up at me and I laughed. "How germ-phobic are you?" he asked.

"Why?" I drew that out into more than one syllable. That was not a question I wanted to answer blindly.

Adam took a sip from one of the cups and nodded. "Because that one's the juice."

I laughed again as he handed it to me. "Thanks."

His lips had left a saliva print on the edge of the cup. I wanted to wipe it off, but that seemed like it might come across as offensive. I rolled the cup between my hands instead, turning the opposite side to face me.

Adam sat back down next to me. He leaned back, and stretched out his legs too. I hadn't noticed before, but he was wearing his sneakers instead of dress shoes.

I kicked his foot. "I wish I'd thought of that."

He lifted up his feet, peering at them, then glanced over at my shoes again. "Yeah. These are far more practical."

I laughed. "I'm not sure Amber and Jenny are familiar with the term practical."

I rubbed at my eye, then stopped as I realised I'd be smearing my makeup. My fingertip held a mix of black eyeliner and sparkly turquoise eyeshadow. I ran my knuckle under my eye, hoping that would remove the worst of my panda impression.

I wondered if I should apologise for bringing up Clare, or if that would just make things worse again. It seemed weird to leave it hanging, but I didn't want to draw more attention to it either.

I sipped at my juice. I had a feeling Adam had had more than one drink inside. He seemed relaxed now, but maybe too much. He laughed louder than usual, and the grin was fixed, rather switching back and forth between smiles and the frown which wasn't a frown.

"So, is Tilly going to follow in your footsteps as a competitive swimmer?" he asked.

I shook my head. "Not likely. She really can't swim." I laughed, thinking of Tilly's arms-and-legs-everywhere version of doggy paddle in a race. "I'm not competing anymore, anyway," I added.

Adam opened his mouth, but I got in before he could ask. Surely the answer was obvious? I'd missed months of training, and it would take me many months more to get up to speed again. "What about you? Why'd you really quit?" I patted his stomach. "Too many fish burgers?"

He caught my hand. "Hey! I didn't quit, I retired, thank you very much."

"At thirteen?"

He shrugged. "Early retirement."

He kept hold of my hand using it to gesture, as he talked. It was kind of cute, except I'm not sure he realised he was doing it. He kept sipping from his cup, and I could see the effect getting stronger each time he raised it to his lips.

"Are you sure you don't want to dance?" he asked me after a while.

I nodded. "I'm sure."

"Come on. Just one dance."

I shook my head. "I thought you didn't want to either."

"Not in there." Adam stood, and pulled me to my feet. "Out here's different."

The music was loud enough, coming straight through the walls of the dining hall. Adam wrapped his arms around me, and we swayed for a moment in an awkward slow dance. It was strange to be this close to him. Perhaps we weren't really any closer than we had been before, sitting next to each other, but it felt different. Not good different. Uncomfortable different. I felt myself closing off, pulling away from him in my head if not for real.

"Bailey ..." Adam stumbled slightly, and I caught his arm. "Wow, you can't balance in those heels, can you?" he said.

"Or maybe you can't balance in all that alcohol?" I pushed him back towards the step. "Sit down, before you do yourself some damage."

I backed away as I said it, folding my arms across my body. I stared into the trees, as if I were fascinated by something there, and not just avoiding looking at him. He was watching me though, I could tell.

He was still for a moment, then he sat back down. "Fine. No dancing. I'm not drunk, though."

"No?" I turned my face towards him, but didn't quite meet his eye.

He shook his head. "No."

He might not have been completely wasted, but he was definitely feeling the effects of the spiked juice. I shifted as I realised I was feeling the effects of the juice too, even if mine hadn't been spiked.

I gestured towards the hall. "I'm just going to go pee." I blushed as I realised there were probably a million better ways of phrasing that. Adam started to laugh and I hurried inside before he could say anything.

I pressed my hands to my temples as soon as I was inside. My pulse pounded under them, and I had to fight the urge to run and escape to the pool.

The atmosphere inside the hall was much quieter now. The music was slow, and couples swayed back and forth in the centre of the room. I felt myself swaying in time too, and let the rhythm leech the embarrassment from me.

I smiled as I saw Amber and Jenny dancing together, Jenny's head tucked against Amber's shoulder.

Eddie was sitting by himself at the side of the hall. I looked around and spotted Clare, swaying on the dance floor with another guy, his arms wrapped close around her. Eddie wasn't watching her, though. He was staring across to the other side of the hall, where Freya sat by herself.

I walked over to him. "Go over there."

He looked up at me. "To Clare? But–"

I shook my head. "Freya." I nodded towards her.

Eddie frowned. He stared at the floor in front of him.

I sighed. "Just ask her to dance. You don't even have to talk to her."

I hoped he didn't take that too literally. I wasn't sure Freya would take kindly to complete silence. He'd probably be okay, though, once they'd got past the first awkwardness.

Eddie looked up at me. The light glinted off his glasses, so I couldn't figure out his expression. I wanted to ask him why he'd gone with Clare in the first place, when it was so obvious he really liked Freya. But asking about Clare hadn't exactly done me any favours tonight.

He sighed, and looked back down at the floor again.

I walked away. Matchmaking was difficult, when the matches wouldn't co-operate.

There was a long line for the girls' loo. I leaned against the wall as I waited. The tinfoil petals had surprisingly sharp edges, and I felt them scratching at my arm. I turned around so my back was against the wall instead.

I was glad I hadn't left it to the last minute, as it seemed like it was going to be a long wait. A girl joined the queue behind me, and she was jiggling she was so desperate.

"Go ahead of me," I said.

She smiled at me. "Thanks."

I shrugged. "You're still going to be waiting a while." No-one else seemed to be willing to give up their place for her.

Eddie and Freya were dancing when I came back out. I smiled at her, but she wrinkled her nose to show things weren't entirely going smoothly. I made what I hoped looked like a sympathy smile in return.

It was a little chilly outside now. Adam had been right about it getting cold at night. During the day I felt like I was only a minute away from heatstroke most of the time, but once the sun went down and the wind picked up it was hard not to shiver.

Adam wasn't where I'd left him. I wandered around the side of the dining hall, then back the other way when I couldn't see him. The south side of the hall was pretty dark. The trees had grown in close, making an arch reaching over to the side of the building.

The windows on this side of the hall were high up and far apart. They cut slices of light into the trees, making shadows fall in uneven chunks.

I opened my mouth to call Adam's name, but stopped as I heard voices.

"I should go." I recognised Adam's voice, and a girl's soft breathy laugh.

"Why?" Clare's voice, unmistakable. "Why rush off, when we're having fun?"

I saw them then, their figures close together in among the shadows. She leaned in to him, and I saw him dip his face to meet hers.

I stepped backwards. They looked up as the leaves crackled under my foot. It was too dark to see their expressions, but they both went still. I turned away before they could react.

Eleven

D AD TOLD ME IT WAS love at first sight between him and Mum. She told a different story.

They met in the surf at a beach. Mum said that was why I was a swimmer – they'd predestined it the first moment they saw each other.

I don't know how old they were. I tried to work it out once, but even though I knew the date of their wedding, I didn't know how long they were engaged, how long they dated before that, or how long it was before he finally worked up the courage to ask her out.

Dad said it was love at first sight. Mum said she tolerated him until he grew on her.

• • • •

I REALISED MY EARRING was missing as I walked away from the dance. I ran my hand through my hair, hoping it was just caught. But it was gone.

"Hey Bailey, wait!"

I hesitated, then let Adam catch up with me. He slowed down as I stopped, obviously more eager to chase after me than he was to actually talk to me. I turned when he was a few paces from me, and walked past him, back towards the dining hall.

"I've lost my earring," I said.

Adam trailed after me. "I'm sorry."

"What for?" I asked. I started searching the ground below the deck where we'd been sitting.

The rhythm of Adam's steps changed as he faltered. "For before ... with Clare."

I shook my head. "It doesn't matter. We're just friends, right? You can kiss Clare if you want." The earring had to be there, it couldn't be gone.

Adam touched my arm, making me stop my pathetic search. I stood up, but didn't look at him. The wind was picking up, and I had to fight against shivers as goose bumps rose on my arms.

"I'm sorry," he said again.

I shrugged. I didn't want to cry in front of him, but if I didn't get back to the cabins soon, I would. "I ..." I forced myself to look at him, but then I had to look away as my eyes watered. I shook my head. "I need to find my earring."

He sighed, and dropped his hand from my arm. He turned away, staring up at the sky. "Me and Clare, it's–"

"Complicated."

He jerked his head, looking at me. I met his eye for a second, then dropped my gaze. His face was pained, like the word was a weapon I'd used against him. Finally he nodded. "Complicated."

I swished my foot back and forth in the dirt, making a colourless rainbow. My feet ached from standing in Amber's heels. I wanted to step out of them, and leave them on the ground next to Adam as he struggled for words.

"I wish ..."

I looked up at him, but he was back to staring at the sky. "I like you, Bailey. You're ..."

I waited, but he didn't finish that either. Uncomplicated, that's what I was, really. I wasn't as bold and exciting as Clare, but I wasn't complicated. It's sad when the girl covered in scars is the simpler option.

Adam lowered his gaze, meeting my eye again. "I wish I'd met you first," he said.

I stared at him. He really meant that, I think. But it wasn't enough. I walked away.

"Bailey?" Adam called, but didn't follow me.

I turned to face him, but kept walking away. "Goodnight, Adam," I said, then I turned my back on him.

• • • •

I PLACED THE ONE EARRING back in my sponge bag. The hook glinted at me, and the feathers splayed out like they would try to creep out when I wasn't looking. "Peacock feathers are bad luck," I said to myself. My mum had been superstitious. She'd also been full of contradictions.

I fought the urge to throw the earring in the bin. They weren't expensive ones. I'd probably be able to find a replacement for the missing one, if I wanted to. It wouldn't be the same, though.

I took the bracelet off and shoved it in the bag. I'd put the photo of Mum and Dad in there too, knowing no-one would look there. Sad, really. I guess it shows you don't have much confidence in the people around you, when you have to hide things with your toothbrush just to keep them private.

I was in bed when Freya, Amber and Jenny arrived. They came in chattering, and I sat up as they put the light on.

"Ooo ... you snuck off early, Bailey."

"Yeah, I had a headache." I rubbed my temple, in the hope of making that more believable. I couldn't face dissecting the black hole that was Clare and Adam's relationship again. My head was pretty sore anyway, and had been for most of the summer.

Amber frowned. She flicked off the main light, turning on Freya's lamp instead. I leant back against my pillow as the three of them sat down on Freya's bed. Well, Amber and Freya sat down. Jenny stumbled, and ended up collapsing over Freya's lap.

Amber pulled her upright. "Sorry, she's had too much 'juice.'"

"I swear I didn't know it was spiked!"

Amber rolled her eyes at me. "She was the one who spiked it."

I forced a smile as Amber settled Jenny back across the bed. Jenny closed her eyes, and her head rolled to the side. Amazingly, she managed to make it look graceful. The curve of her arm cradled her head, as if she were posed there, not just passed out.

Amber sighed. "Sorry, Freya, I'll get her out of here in a minute."

Freya nodded. She pinched at the fabric of her dress, making it fluff out around her. It was the pink floaty dress Amber had wanted me to try on first. It would have washed me out, but on Freya it looked gorgeous.

"You didn't get to talk to Eddie tonight?" I asked her.

She shook her head. "Not really. He did dance with me a couple of times, but he didn't say anything."

I bit my tongue, knowing that was probably my fault. I didn't mention my conversation with him, though.

"He was looking at you the whole night, you know," I said instead. I didn't know if that was true, since I'd been outside most of the time, but it probably was. It was clear as anything he'd regretted going with Clare instead of Freya. "He looked bored to tears by Clare," I added.

Freya stared at me, then shook her head. "It doesn't matter. He still went with her instead of me."

I nodded. I knew the feeling.

Freya stood, undoing her necklace and draping it over the head of the bed. It held for a second, then slowly slithered down the other side with a hiss. It clattered as it hit the floor behind the bed.

"Dammit!" Freya knelt on her mattress to lean over and peer at it, then thumped back down on the bed. "I'll get it tomorrow."

Amber looked from me to Freya. She rubbed her hand over Jenny's arm, but Jenny didn't stir.

Amber jerked her head towards the door. "I'd better get Jenny to bed. Freya, can you give me a hand?"

Freya closed her eyes in a deep sigh. "All right." She kicked her heels off and stood up again.

"I'd get up and help," I said, "but ..." I trailed off as I tried to think of a plausible reason why I couldn't. "I'm too comfortable," I said finally. I pulled the blanket up to cover the lower half of my face as I started laughing.

Amber shook her head. "Slacker."

Amber and Freya managed to haul Jenny upright, but her head lolled against Amber's shoulder and she mumbled something incomprehensible.

"God, I'm never letting her drink again."

I sighed, realising I probably would have to get up and help. But then the door opened and Tilly came in, saving me from having to offer. She stopped as she saw the other girls.

"Come on, bub." I pulled the covers back to let her climb into the bed.

"What's wrong with Jenny?" Tilly asked me, as she clambered up.

Amber shot me a look. "She's just ... not feeling well."

Tilly stared at Jenny, then scrunched up her nose. "I know what drunk is, Amber," she said.

Amber laughed. "All right, then. She's drunk as a skunk, and a little more to boot."

I tickled Tilly. "See, Tilly? This is why you shouldn't drink until you're very old. You look silly and people have to carry you around."

"I'll help you get her into the other room," Freya said.

Between them, they managed to manoeuvre Jenny towards the door. Amber looked back at me when they got to the doorway, and it seemed like she wanted to say something else, then Jenny groaned and raised her head.

"Come on, babe." Amber stroked Jenny's forehead. "We're taking you to bed."

Jenny swayed, and Amber had to wrap her arms around her to stop her toppling over. She coughed, and rubbed her face. "I wish we could have gone to the dance together," she said to Amber. "Like properly together." She leaned her head back down on Amber's shoulder. Her face was lit from the lamp, but Amber's was still in shadow. They swayed slightly, and the light moved back and forth over Amber's neck, casting kiwifruit-spiky hair shadows.

I stared at Amber, but she didn't meet my eye. Freya did, though, and she looked like she didn't know what to say.

"Can you open the door, Freya?" Amber said eventually. She shuffled Jenny out of the room without looking back at me.

• • • •

I GOT UP EARLY THE next morning, and went for a swim. There were a couple of people hanging around, but I didn't worry about them. I pushed myself harder and faster, making up for the days' training I'd missed.

When I surfaced, Adam was standing by the fence watching me. I met his eye for a moment, then dived and swam another set of lengths. When I broke the surface again, he was gone.

I stared up at the sky, as it started to spit. Everything was turning grey and miserable. I ducked my head under the water again, then pulled myself out to face it.

Tilly talked to me as we walked down to the dining hall for breakfast. I wasn't really concentrating, though, and I heard Freya pick up the other half of the conversation.

Freya touched my shoulder as we joined the queue. "Are you okay?"

I looked up at her. "Yeah, I'm fine. Why?"

She glanced over her shoulder. "Amber told me what happened last night."

"Amber? How did she ...?" I stopped myself. Clare told her, of course. I shook my head. "I'm fine. Adam and I weren't together, so ..." So I didn't really have a right to be upset. Part of me wished we had been together. Not because it would have changed anything, but because then at least I wouldn't have to pretend not to be hurt.

"Still," Freya said. She made a face at Clare's back as we passed her.

I forced a smile. "I just feel sorry for her roommate."

Freya frowned. "Didn't you hear? She was in with Louise, but they had some kind of blow out and Louise asked to change." Freya rolled her eyes. "So of course Clare ended up with a cabin to herself."

I wasn't sure I'd ever talked to Louise, but I'd seen her a couple of times at the pool and in the dining hall. As far as I could remember she'd seemed pretty nice, but I'd thought that about Clare too, at first. There was probably a lot more to their "blow out" than they were letting on.

"Must be kind of lonely," I said, then shook my head. Most likely Clare had messed with Louise in some way, like she had with everyone else. She didn't deserve my sympathy.

• • • •

THAT NIGHT I WENT TO bed before everything started with the prank. Amber and Jenny had told me what they were planning, but I wasn't paying much attention. I gathered it involved making a bucketful of custard that was going to end up on someone's head, but the logistics sounded a bit dodgy. I'm not sure if they had it figured out either, or if they were just caught up in the idea that it would be funny whether or not they knew how to achieve it.

I peered out of the window as they left. The wind was really picking up, and the clouds had finally broken. The spitting had turned to full-on rain, and my guess was it would get heavier as the night wore on.

Freya hung back with me. They had gone with the idea of pranking Eddie, and I could tell she wasn't in the mood to be involved. I glanced over at her a couple of times, but she had her headphones on and her face to the wall.

When Tilly arrived, she was soaked from the rain. I borrowed Jenny's hairdryer and blasted her with it, making her giggle and squirm away from me.

We all had hopelessly inadequate pyjamas – singlets and shorts, nothing warm at all. We snuggled down under all the blankets I could find, and I read Tilly a story by the light of my cell phone. Freya didn't turn over, but I noticed she took her headphones out when I started reading.

The rain grew heavier, beating against the roof of the cabin.

Freya glanced over her shoulder at me. "Eddie won't even need to wash the custard off with all this," she said.

I looked down at Tilly. She'd drifted off, her head rolling against my arm.

Freya smiled, and lowered her voice. "I talked to him today."

"Yeah?"

She nodded. "He said he wished he'd asked me to the dance instead of going with Clare." She leant her head back down on the pillow, staring at the ceiling. "It's kind of too late, though. Regrets are all well and good, but–"

I shook my head. "Give it a couple of days. See how you feel then."

Freya looked over at me. "Do you feel differently about Adam?"

I frowned. "It's not the same thing." I stared at the ceiling too. I wondered how it would hold up against the storm. This place seemed built for summer only, and I wouldn't have been surprised if everything started leaking at the first hint of weather.

"It's not?"

I shook my head. "We weren't together, so ..." I tilted my head to look at Freya. I hesitated, wondering if it was actually worth voicing the thoughts that had been going around in my head. "Even without Clare, every time Adam and I got close, and it seemed like something was going to happen, it was ..." I shook my head. "I felt so awkward."

Freya rolled her eyes and scoffed. "That just means you like him, Bailey."

I frowned. "Maybe." I wasn't convinced. I'd never felt like that around David, even right at the beginning. But David and I were hardly the benchmark of a good relationship.

Freya made a noise in her throat. "I don't get Clare," she said. "And I really don't get Eddie for going with her."

I sighed. After everything that had happened, I didn't feel any obligation to keep Clare's secrets. "No-one asked Clare to go to the dance. That's why she asked Eddie," I said quietly. "I think ... I think Clare has some issues." I stopped short of telling Freya about Josh in the bushes, though. Or about the vomiting.

Freya turned over to look at me. She frowned. "That doesn't explain why he said yes."

I shrugged. "Maybe he thought you'd say no." It was always easier to be the one answering than the one asking. I'd figured it out later. Clare was too scared to ask Adam, in case he said no.

She'd probably hoped he would ask her, but when she found out he'd asked me instead she'd panicked.

Freya stared at me, then finally nodded. "A couple of days. Maybe we'll both change our minds."

I looked down at Tilly. She was well and truly asleep now. I set down the book and turned out the light on my cell phone.

• • • •

I WOKE AS THE LIGHT of a torch flashed against the window. For a moment I was back in my bed at home, with the car headlights flashing across my bedroom wall.

I relaxed as my eyes adjusted, taking in the walls of the cabin and Freya's sleeping form in the bed opposite.

The rain was still heavy against the roof, but I could hear something else in among it – voices, maybe two of them, talking and giggling on the deck outside our cabin.

I half sat up, trying to see out the window without waking Tilly. "Hello?" I said.

The voices stopped, and the torch light flickered out. I held my breath, waiting, but everything was quiet. I sighed, and settled back against the pillow. Perhaps it was Clare, meeting up with some other poor unsuspecting guy. I had half a mind to go out there and warn him what he was getting into. I turned over, tucking up against Tilly instead.

The door burst open. Several people flooded into the room, all of them yelling. Freya sat up and screamed. I sat up too, but I didn't scream. "What the–?"

I doubled over as Tilly kicked me in the stomach. "Tilly," I gasped.

I reached for her, but my hand closed on nothing. Someone grabbed me, pulling me out of bed. Another threw a pillowcase over my head. I screamed, kicking and hitting out as hard as I could. My foot connected with someone, and they swore. The arms disappeared from around me, and I was on the floor.

I'd landed on my tailbone. Pain shot up my spine as I tried to stand. I tried to rip off the pillowcase, but hands grabbed my shoulders before I could. I scrambled to get my feet underneath me.

"Let go of me!" My voice was lost in the noise. "Please, my sister!" They held me down, pouring what smelt like baked beans over me. I struggled against the hands holding me, but I couldn't break free.

"Tilly!" I screamed. I couldn't hear if she answered.

• • • •

I REMEMBER HEARING the ambulance siren, and forcing myself to open my eyes. Tilly was lying curled up next to my side. I don't know whether she turned me over onto my back, or whether I rolled over at some point before she came downstairs.

"Tilly?" I said. It came out as a whisper. I felt her stir, but she didn't say anything.

She'd called the ambulance. She never said anything about that afterwards, but the police told me it was her voice on the emergency line recording.

I don't know what it was that had made her hide in the wardrobe. The glass in the back door being smashed, maybe, or possibly Mum made some kind of sound. Whatever it was, I slept through it, but Tilly heard it and was scared enough to hide. The fact that she did probably saved her life. And mine.

I remember closing my eyes, because it hurt too much to keep them open.

Tilly must have seen everything. Mum slumped on the couch, her skull cracked by the blow to the back of her head. Dad on the stairs, where he'd fallen and broken his neck.

And me, on the kitchen floor, bleeding from the stab wound in my stomach.

She must have had to climb over Dad, but she never spoke about that either. She came downstairs when it was quiet, and phoned the ambulance.

Then she lay on the floor next to me, until it came. The weight of her body, putting pressure on the wound, was the only reason I was still alive.

My little sister had saved my life.

Twelve

MY BREATH WAS coming out in short gasps. It didn't feel like I was getting any air. The noise and laughter continued, and the hands finally released me.

There were baked beans mashed under my palms, baked beans everywhere. I tried to get up, but my feet slid in the mess. Freya was still screaming. I wanted to tell her to shut up. The laughter from the guys started to peter out.

Someone pulled the pillowcase from my head, and Adam stared down at me. "Bailey? Oh my god. This was supposed to be Amber's cabin!" He crouched down beside me. "Are you okay? Are you hurt?"

He pulled me upright and tried to wipe some of the gunk off me. I saw Amber and Jenny crowding in the doorway. They were in summer pyjamas too, and they shivered in the cold.

I pushed Adam away. "Tilly," I said. "Where's Tilly?" I couldn't see her.

"She was in here?" Adam started swearing then, and didn't stop. Amber pressed her hand to her mouth.

I stood, using the side of the bed for support. "Tilly!" My voice rose, panic flooding me. "Oh my god, where is she?" The door had been wide open. She thought we were being attacked, she must have run.

I went for the door, but I slipped again. Eddie and Josh both reached out, Eddie's hand closing around my arm.

"Don't touch me!" I shoved him away. I was surprised at how steady my voice was. It was low and gravelly, not like my voice at all.

Adam took my elbow, helping me through the baked beans. "Freya, stay here in case she comes back. Amber, go up to the office and tell them what's happened. Jenny, check the bathrooms and the other cabins. Everyone else, pair up and go look for her."

I went for the doorway again, but Clare was standing in it, barring my way.

She rubbed her face. "God, what's the drama? You don't need to wake everyone up just for one prank." She smirked at me.

I punched her in the face, as hard as I could. Adam grabbed my shoulder, trying to stop me, and I slapped him, leaving a tomato-sauce print on his skin. He backed away, his hand raised to his cheek. He'd done that once before. When our hands were cold at the camp fire. He stared at me, but I turned away.

Clare clutched at her nose. "What's wrong with you, you psycho?"

"You did this," I screamed. "She's out there alone because of you."

Eddie stepped between us, clearly afraid I'd hit her again.

Clare shook her head. "What the hell is she talking about?"

I didn't answer. I bolted for the door. "Tilly!" I yelled. My voice disappeared in the storm. "Tilly!" I ran towards the trees. Would she head for Gran's? Or to the kids' area? I didn't know.

"Tilly!" I screamed again.

I checked the bushes, searching for any sign she was hiding in them. She would be freezing. I was soaked through already, and I'd been outside less than a minute. Behind me, lights came on in the buildings. Torch beams cut through the trees, and I could hear the broken-up sounds of other people calling her name too.

"She'll be scared of anyone else," I said out loud. Then I screamed her name again.

I was shaking, I realised, and crying. "Tilly," I said, but it didn't come out very loud. I spun around on the spot, not knowing which way to go next.

A light flashed in my face, blinding me. I raised my hand, shielding my eyes.

"Bailey?" The beam flicked away, and Adam stepped forward. He gripped my wrist as if he thought I might run again. "Put this on."

I stared at him, not understanding until he bent my arm, forcing it into the sleeve of a jacket. It was Freya's, not mine, and it had been hanging on the back of the door. I pulled it on over my soaking, tomato-sauce drenched pyjamas.

"And these." He handed me a pair of shoes. My feet were sinking into the mud, my toes disappearing. They squelched as I slipped them into the shoes.

"I need to find her," I said.

He nodded. "We will."

"She'll be scared of anyone else," I added. My voice had gone quiet, as the meaning of my own words sunk in.

Adam nodded again. He put his arm around me, guiding me back the way he'd come. "Amber thought she saw her back this way," he said. He aimed the light from his phone in front of our feet, but the beam disappeared into the night. All I could see were flashes of gold and silver as it caught the rain.

I stumbled, and he gripped my shoulder tighter.

"Keep calling out," he said. "She'll come back if she hears your voice."

I stared at him, barely able to understand what he was saying.

"Go on," he said.

I looked out at the path in front of us. "Tilly?" I called. It didn't come out very loud, so I cleared my throat and said it again louder. "Tilly!"

I slowed my steps, holding my breath and my muscles tight as I listened. "I think ..." I scanned the area in front of us. For a second, I'd thought I heard her.

"What is it?" Adam flashed the light back and forth in front of us.

"Tilly?" I called again.

I took off running as I heard it again. Tilly calling out my name. Adam kept up with me. "Tilly?" he yelled. His voice was louder than mine, echoing in the air.

Around us there were other lights, other voices calling out Tilly's name. I couldn't hear her in among all of them.

"Where are we?" I asked Adam.

He flashed the light around again. "By the equipment shed. Near the pool."

The pool. "Oh my god." I started to run again. "Oh my god. She's at the pool," I screamed to Adam.

Tilly wouldn't go to Gran's or back to the kids' area. She'd go to find me. She'd think I'd go to the pool, because that's where I always went.

I stumbled as I ran. It was so dark. Tilly would fall and she wasn't as strong as me in the water. She'd only ever learned to not drown.

Adam picked up his pace, running ahead of me.

"Tilly!" I screamed.

I heard her shriek and the splash as she hit the water from where we were. Against the rain, it was just a tiny sound, like a bird's cry. I tried to make myself keep moving, but my legs sunk under me. Ahead of me I saw Adam scrambling over the fence, the phone going flying as he did.

"Tilly," I tried to say, but there was no sound. I held my head in my hands.

I heard Dad's voice in my head, scolding me for cutting myself off from them by diving under the water. I remembered why he said it now. It was because Tilly wanted to go with me to the pool, and I wouldn't let her. I didn't want to have to look after her, like I always looked after her. I couldn't even have a room to myself because she sleep-walked. That's why I liked swimming so much, because Tilly couldn't do it.

The outside lighting came on, blinding me again. I saw Adam pulling Tilly out of the pool, but I couldn't get up. I just sat there watching, like it was all already over.

Tilly was moving, though, fighting against Adam, trying to get away from him. I stood, walking over to them. Then running as my brain kicked in.

Adam passed her over the fence to me. She clung to my neck as soon as she was in my arms. "I want Mummy!" she screamed. "I want Mummy and Daddy."

I stared at Adam. "She didn't drown," I said.

He shook his head. "She'd only just gone in. I ..." He trailed off as I closed my eyes.

I sat down on the ground, hugging Tilly to me. "I'm so sorry," I whispered to her. She just kept screaming, asking for Mum and Dad.

"They're gone, bub," I said.

"The men!" she screamed. "The men came back."

I didn't know what she meant, then I grabbed her face, making her look at me. "No," I said.

She scrunched up her eyes, but I kept holding her. "It wasn't them, Tilly. It was just a stupid prank. They weren't going to hurt us."

"The man with the tattoo," she screamed. "I saw the man with the tattoo."

"Tattoo?" I looked at Adam. "Who has a tattoo?"

Adam shook his head. "Lots of the guys. I don't know."

"The one who hit Mummy."

"Hit Mummy ..." I repeated Tilly's words without understanding them. I stared at Adam. His bottom lip dropped, and he looked like he wanted to vomit. It was that, more than what Tilly had said, that made me understand.

My throat felt like it was closing up, but I forced myself to keep talking. "The one who ... He had a tattoo? That night, did you see the man who ...?" I couldn't keep going. I covered my mouth.

"He came back!"

My stomach clenched at the thought, the need to run away strong. I shook my head. Tilly needed more than that, but I couldn't find the words. The man who stabbed me couldn't have been in the cabin, could he? I started shaking again and squeezed her tighter to ground myself.

"No," I said finally. It had to just be Tilly's memory; it made no sense for him to have been there. "It wasn't him, Tilly." I forced myself to breathe again.

She'd seen it. She'd seen everything. That's why she hid. I searched in my mind for a tattoo on the guy who stabbed me, but there was still only a blank space. All I could see was the knife and the glass.

I pulled Tilly closer to me. "It was just Adam and his friends playing a prank, Tilly. Some of them have tattoos." I don't think she heard me, so I kept talking. To myself as much as to her. "You're safe, Tilly. It wasn't the same man. I'll keep you safe."

"Bailey?"

I heard Adam, but I couldn't think about anything except Tilly. He said my name a couple more times, then crouched down beside me when I didn't move. He reached to take Tilly from me. I pulled her away from him, burying my face in her hair.

"We should take her back to the cabins," he said.

"No." I shook my head. "I'm taking her to Gran's."

Adam swallowed, and let his hands falls to his sides. I couldn't look at him. I couldn't look at anything except Tilly.

"Do you want me to go?" he asked. His voice was low, and he stared at the ground.

My breath caught, and I felt my chest contract. I gripped his arm. "Please don't." I was hurting him, I think, as his muscles tensed under my hand, but I couldn't let go. "Please don't leave me alone."

Adam took my hand, peeling it from his arm and gripping it in his own.

"It's okay, Bailey," he said, repeating my words to Tilly. "You're safe."

Thirteen

I LOST TILLY IN A MALL when I was twelve. Mum always said it was her fault; that I'd been too young for such responsibility. It wasn't true, though. I knew it was my fault and I'd never forgiven myself for it.

Tilly had been dawdling and I'd got mad at her. So I walked off without her, assuming she'd follow. There was some T-shirt I'd been saving up to buy, and I just couldn't wait another five minutes for my little sister to catch up.

It was fifteen minutes or more before I realised she was missing.

We found her in a bookshop, trying to read a picture book. I felt so bad, I bought her the book with the money I'd saved for the T-shirt.

• • • •

GRAN GAVE US SOME DRY clothes. I dressed Tilly like I would a baby, pulling the clothes over her head as she cried. I didn't tell her to stop. She could cry as much as she needed now.

Adam was waiting in the lounge when I came out. I stared at him, but didn't say anything. He was still in his wet clothes, and stood in the middle of the floor, a circle of water appearing on the floor around him as he dripped.

Gran disappeared into the kitchen, and we could hear her clattering pans. Tilly was still crying, but quietly now. She muttered things into my shoulder. I couldn't understand what she was saying. I heard the words "Mummy and Daddy" several times, though.

The resort's nurse and some of the other staff appeared, but Tilly wouldn't let them touch her. I didn't want to talk to them either. I pulled Tilly into my lap and stared at the wall, until they gave up and left.

"I should have checked," Adam said. "Clare said Amber and Freya were in that cabin, and–"

"They were," I said. My voice came out flat and hollow. "Except I switched with Amber, because she wanted to be in with Jenny."

Adam went still. "So Clare didn't–"

"She knew."

Adam sagged as I said that. I pulled Tilly closer. I wasn't sure whether Clare had known Tilly was sleeping in my bed, but she'd definitely known I was in that cabin. I could tell Adam desperately wanted to be able to let her off the hook, but she'd done it on purpose; there was no doubt in my mind about that.

Gran came back in with a mug of Milo. "Come on, Tilly," she said. "This will help you sleep."

Tilly didn't look up until I lifted her chin and put the mug in her hands. "Drink it, Tilly."

I had to cup my hands around the mug to stop her spilling it. Her hands were shaking, and she muttered between mouthfuls. I was shaking too, and my muscles hurt they were so tight. I couldn't relax. I couldn't make my heart stop hammering.

Tilly fell asleep before she was finished, her head drooping against my arm. Adam took the mug from me, and I laid Tilly down on the couch.

Gran went into the kitchen again, and came back with a bottle of brandy. I suspected she'd added a shot of it to Tilly's Milo, wanting to calm her enough to make her sleep. She didn't bother with the pretence this time, pouring the brandy straight into glasses. She handed one each to me and Adam.

I swirled the glass then took a sip, holding the liquid in my mouth before swallowing. It burned on the way down, but the warming was good.

"She wanted to go home." My eyes felt wet as I thought about it. "I told her–"

Gran put her arms around me. "It's not your fault, my darling."

"I wouldn't have done it on purpose," Adam said to Gran.

She hesitated, then I felt her nodding. "I don't imagine you would have."

I don't think she knew what he was talking about. I'm not sure if she knew about the prank, either. She knew what had happened tonight, of course, but I don't think she knew why. I'd figured it out, even before Adam said it. The boys had wanted Clare's help with figuring out who was in each cabin, and so she'd lied to make me the target and Tilly had got caught in the middle.

"Tilly saw the man who hit Mum," I said to Gran. "He had a tattoo."

"Oh my god." Gran covered her mouth in the same way I had when I realised. The same way Mum used to when she got a fright.

I could see it running through Gran's head. Tilly had seen the blow that killed Mum. She'd had to climb over Dad's body to reach me. She'd lain on the ground next to me, saving my life with her body.

"So she could ID them?" Gran asked.

"I don't know. She said she saw him hit Mum." I shook my head. "That was all."

· · · ·

I DON'T KNOW IF IT was the brandy, or if I was just exhausted, but I didn't dream at all that night. I woke on Gran's couch next to Tilly, my arm numb from lying so heavily on it.

Tilly didn't stir. Her brow furrowed and her eyes darted under her eyelids, but she didn't wake.

Adam was gone. Gran said he'd stayed, watching me and Tilly sleep, until she made him leave. I didn't know what to say when she told me that.

Freya was still asleep when I got back to the cabins. Eddie was lying on my bed. He sat up as I came in. "I just ..." He looked towards Freya, and I nodded. Everyone had been focused on me and Tilly last night, and no-one else had thought to check whether Freya was okay.

I crept around, collecting my sponge bag and towel, so I wouldn't wake her.

I stood under the shower for even longer than I would normally, scrubbing the last traces of baked beans from my skin and trying to get rid of the chill I still felt. Every time I thought about what Tilly had said, I felt cold.

I didn't bother to dry my hair properly; I just let it drip. My hands were still shaking. I stared at their reflection in the mirror, as if they were someone else's. They didn't seem to be connected to me anymore. Didn't seem to do what I wanted.

My knuckles were bruised from punching Clare. I flexed my hand, watching the reflection and feeling the pain of it. My parents would have been angry at me for hitting her. I was glad I had done it, though, even if that fact alone made me feel guilty.

I turned my hand over, staring at the palm. I wished I hadn't slapped Adam, though.

I picked up my sponge bag, but fumbled and dropped it. I stooped down to pick up the contents.

The single peacock feather earring looked even more like an omen of bad luck than it had the other day. Perhaps I should have thrown it out, when I'd had the impulse the first time. I stared at it, then stuffed it back in the sponge bag.

I picked up my toothbrush and Mum's bracelet, then the photo of Mum and Dad.

I couldn't look at it. I'd been so angry with Tilly for defacing it. I should have made her talk to me about it, instead of letting her hide away like she had every day since that night.

I rubbed my hand over the lines she'd drawn. She must have been so scared last night. It struck me as odd, that I hadn't been frightened myself. I hadn't felt anything until she was gone, and then I'd been terrified.

She must have thought the men had come back to kill us. She'd probably seen one of the guy's tattoos and thought it was the man who ...

I looked down at Tilly's scribbles again. They seemed random. Just a whole load of lines and spirals. But it wasn't random – it was a pattern. The same pattern she'd been drawing over and over obsessively for the past few months. Ever since the night our parents died.

I shoved the photo in my pocket and ran out of the bathroom.

Tilly was awake when I got back up to Gran's. Gran had left a bowl of cereal on the coffee table in front of her, but Tilly hadn't touched it. Gran gave me a tired smile as I came in. She had a newspaper spread out on the table in front of her, but I don't think she was reading it.

I sat down next to Tilly, and put the bowl in her lap. "Eat your breakfast, Till."

Tilly didn't move at first, then I put the spoon in her hand and she started eating. I let her finish it, before I took the photo out of my pocket.

"Why did you draw on Mummy and Daddy's photo, Tilly?" I asked.

"What?" Gran's head shot up from the paper.

I held the photo out to her, but kept my eyes on Tilly.

Gran took it out of my hand. She covered her mouth again as she looked at it. "Tilly did this?"

I nodded. "Why did you draw on the photo, Till?" I asked again.

Tilly tipped her cereal bowl, making the little dribbles of leftover milk move around. Her eyes were shiny. She blinked, and the film of tears spilled over.

"Tilly, tell me why you drew on the photo."

"Bailey, stop it." Gran's face was pale. I couldn't tell whether she was angry with me, or scared by Tilly's silence. It didn't matter either way.

I grabbed the photo off her. "Tilly, look at the photo. Tell me why you drew this."

"Bailey!"

I ignored Gran, keeping my focus on Tilly. "Why did you draw this?"

Tilly's hands were shaking, but she kept tilting her bowl. Making a spiral in the milk.

"This is the tattoo, isn't it?" I pointed at the photo. "You saw this on the man who hit Mummy."

Gran's hand flew to her mouth again. She was crying now too. I couldn't breathe as I watched Tilly. She didn't seem to be breathing either.

I pressed my hands to the sides of her face. "It's okay, Tilly," I whispered. "I won't let them hurt you."

Finally she nodded, just once. My hands jerked too, with the movement of her head, and I felt the wet brush of her eyelid against my fingertips.

"Oh my god." Gran snatched the photo from me and started muttering about ringing the police.

I wrapped my arms around Tilly. "Thank you, bub."

Fourteen

I WENT EARLY TO THE dining room for breakfast. They were just setting up, not really ready for anyone to be arriving, but the chef let me have a bowl of cereal and some coffee when I said I was going home early. I could have eaten at Gran's, but I needed to be away from it for a while. Even if only for the time it took to eat a bowl of cereal.

I was just finishing when other people started arriving.

Jack rushed up to me. "Where's Tilly?" he asked. Adam hovered behind him.

"Tilly's not having breakfast this morning," I said.

Jack seemed to lose confidence in talking to me, as soon he realised Tilly wasn't there. Perhaps his willingness to get over his fear of cooties only extended as far as Tilly. He stared at me for a moment, in that unnerving way kids have. Sometimes it seems like their age lets them see straight through you. I blinked as he ran off to get some food from the buffet. Adam stayed hovering by the table.

"Sit down," I said to him, without looking up.

Adam hesitated, then perched on the edge of the seat. I could feel him watching me, but I kept my focus on my coffee.

"I'm sorry I slapped you," I said.

Adam shrugged. "It's okay." He rubbed his hand against his cheek, but in an absent kind of way, not like it really hurt. "How's Tilly?" he asked.

I shook my head.

"Bailey?"

I glanced up. His index finger tapped against the back of his other hand, and I could feel his leg jiggling beneath the table. He jerked his head towards the door. "Can we ...?"

I swallowed. I wanted to say no. What more was there to say, anyway?

Instead, I nodded. "Sure."

Adam sat down on the steps outside. I hesitated, then joined him, sitting next to him but one step back. The wood was damp against the backs of my legs, having soaked up all the rain from the night. I pulled my knees up, wrapping my arms around them.

"We're going home. This afternoon," I said.

Adam looked up at me, and his lips parted.

"Tilly's ... we should have made her stay in counselling. Things are ..." I shook my head. "It's just too big for her to deal with."

"Are *you* okay?" he asked.

I shrugged. It was a strange question. No, I wasn't "okay". But I wasn't that bad. Better than Tilly, at least. I shook my head. "I don't know."

I'd been thinking about it so much lately. Everything that had happened the night my parents died. I wondered if that was why I hadn't been scared last night; I'd used up all my fear going over and over it in my head. I'd panicked when I thought Tilly was gone, but the rest of it? Maybe part of me had known it wasn't really a threat.

Adam glanced back at me. "I'm really sorry."

There was a gruffness to his voice, almost like he thought I wouldn't believe him. I opened my mouth to say something, but he got in first.

"Clare ..."

I shook my head, but he continued anyway.

"It's like, if she's not the centre of attention, for even five minutes ..." He shook his head. "She just loses it. Creates all this drama, for nothing." Adam turned to face me. He stared at me like he was waiting for me to say I understood.

"I think ..." I swallowed. My throat felt so dry. "Clare has problems. You can't take responsibility for her." I wondered if I should tell him what I knew. Did anyone else know about the self-destructive things Clare was doing to herself, or was it just me? I didn't want to be burdened with that responsibility.

Adam lowered his gaze. He scratched at his face, rubbing sleep from under his eyes. I shifted again, to make myself more comfortable. I'm not sure if what I said would make any difference to him. It seemed like Adam would spend the rest of his life revolving around Clare, trying to convince himself she wasn't a bad person.

He cleared his throat. "Did she tell you why we broke up?"

I shrugged. "I got a couple of different versions."

Adam nodded, like he wasn't surprised by that. He stared straight ahead, crinkling up his eyes as he squinted. "I have an older brother. Did I tell you that?"

I looked up at him. "Yeah," I said. "Michael, right?"

Adam nodded and pressed his fingertips against the bridge of his nose. "Mike. He used to come here every year, but he's at university now." He stopped, and rubbed his head with his hand. I glanced up, as it started to spit. I shivered, but Adam made no move to go back inside.

He ran his tongue over his lower lip. "I don't know if I ever really liked her," he said, but it was quiet. To himself, not to me.

"She's not very likeable." He almost laughed as he said it, as if he was just realising.

I wondered if that was in answer to my question at the dance, about whether he still liked Clare. If it was, I think he was kidding himself.

I swallowed. I thought of Adam's anger when Jack first brought up their older brother. "So I presume Clare ..." I faltered, not quite sure if there was a tactful way of saying what I was thinking.

Adam nodded. "We had a fight at the dance, and I went down to her cabin afterwards to talk to her. Found Mike in her bed." He leaned his head back and stared at the sky. "He was so drunk; I don't think he knew what he was doing. But she ..." He shook his head.

The spitting grew heavier, turning into proper rain again. I glanced at Adam, then moved up a couple of steps so I was sheltered by the veranda. After a second, he joined me. He sat next to me this time, his arm pressing against mine. I shifted away, giving myself some space.

"I didn't want to come back here this year," Adam said, "but Mike and I never told Mum what happened." He sighed and ran his hands through his hair. "I just didn't realise how hard it would be, seeing her again."

I nodded. "She knows how to push your buttons."

Adam looked at me sharply, then nodded. "Yeah, that's exactly what it is."

I rubbed my legs, brushing off the stray raindrops. The rain, like everything, was warm, so it wasn't too much of a problem. But the wind was picking up, making goose bumps rise on my legs where the water evaporated.

"So what about you?" Adam asked.

"Huh?" I looked up at him.

He shifted. "Clare said there was a guy. Back home." He raised his hands into air quotes. "'Complicated,' she said."

I shook my head. "Not that kind of complicated." I shrugged. I wondered how Clare even knew about it. I'd told the other girls, but apart from saying I had an ex, I hadn't told Clare anything about David. Maybe she'd just made it up.

Adam was still waiting for an answer, so I continued with the edited version. "He couldn't really cope with everything that had happened. He's seeing someone else now." I didn't tell him the part about it being my best friend. That part *was* complicated, but even then, not that much. I left a lot of that behind when I moved to Gran's, and by now none of it really mattered to me.

Adam frowned. "But, Clare said ..." He groaned, squeezing the sides of his face with his hands. "She lies about everything!"

I shrugged again and swallowed. Would it have made a difference if he'd known I was single? Probably not. Clare would still have found a way to mess things up. And Tilly would still have been struggling. Really, she should have been my priority all along. Not Adam.

"I should get going." I stood up.

Adam looked up at me, his face crumpling into a deep frown. He stood too, slowly.

I thought about saying I'd miss him, that it had been good getting to know him. I didn't, though. That would just make it harder.

"Well, see you," I said.

"Yeah ..." Adam looked like he wanted to say something else, but I didn't let him. I raised my hand into a wave and walked away.

• • • •

I DAWDLED OVER PACKING up my stuff. It was silly, really, since I'd barely unpacked anything to begin with, but I made collecting up my toiletries and other bits and pieces take as long as possible.

"Are you sure you have to go?" Freya asked me. Again. She'd asked about five times already, just this morning. I think some of my reluctance to leave was because of her reluctance to have me go.

"Yeah, I have to," I said to Freya.

She was still in bed. I'm not sure anyone other than Eddie had checked on her since last night.

"Are you okay?" I asked.

She hesitated, then nodded. "Yeah, I'm fine."

I stared at her, waiting for her to give me the real answer.

She gave me a half smile. "When they came rushing in ... that was the scariest thing that's ever happened to me," she said softly.

I nodded.

"I ... I actually wet myself," she added. She looked embarrassed, and I could tell she regretted saying it.

I hesitated, then nodded. "Tilly did too, I think."

She opened her mouth, like she wanted to ask me something else; probably about my parents. I stepped out onto the deck so she couldn't.

I could hear Amber and Jenny talking inside their cabin. I hadn't seen either of them since yesterday, but I think Freya had told them I was going. I couldn't face telling them myself. It would be like when Tilly and I left for Gran's, all over again.

I went into the bathroom, to make sure I hadn't left anything in there. I knew I hadn't, but the superstitious hold my mother's influence had over me made me check – if I didn't, there would be something in there I'd forgotten.

One of the stall doors was closed, and I heard someone inside throwing up. I hesitated, caught between the urge to flee as if I'd never heard it, and the knowledge that the guilt would follow me if I did.

Clare opened the stall door. Her eyes grew wide as they met mine in the mirror, then she ducked her head and rinsed her mouth out at the sink.

I thought about running back into the cabin and hiding from her until it was time for us to go. Instead I stood my ground, staring at her until she raised her head again. Her nose and eyes were bruised where I'd hit her, and she'd tried to cover it up with makeup.

"I shouldn't have punched you," I said. I didn't apologise, though, and I wouldn't no matter what happened.

She met my eye, totally unashamed, and shrugged. She glanced down at the bag in my hand. "So is it true? You're leaving?"

I nodded. I don't know how she thought I could possibly stay.

She rolled her tongue around her mouth, cleaning her teeth with the tip. "I suppose I owe you an apology."

I shook my head. "If you don't mean it, don't bother."

She shrugged. "Fine then."

I thought about asking her why she did it. But I didn't. I'm not sure she would have given me an answer. She swayed on the spot, letting her arms dangle. I realised suddenly, that I was taller than her. I was probably stronger too, with all the training. She was too thin, her wrists bony and pathetically weak.

"I didn't know she was in there," she said.

I looked back at Clare. She met my eye, then her gaze slid away. "Your sister. I didn't mean for her to be there."

I nodded. That was something, at least. Her eyes were red around the edges, so perhaps she did feel some guilt too.

"I didn't think it would be that big a deal," she said. "But I don't always ... " Now she was talking to herself, more than to me. She rocked back and forth on her heels, then closed her eyes. "Sometimes I don't think things through."

She wanted me to brush it off, just like everyone else did with all the crap she pulled. I thought it was a convention of this place, but it wasn't. It was a convention of Clare. That's why she didn't stop, because no-one ever made her.

I swallowed. "I didn't tell anyone," I said.

Clare looked blank, so I nodded towards the toilet stall. "About you throwing up ... or about Josh." With anyone else, I would have classed those two incidents as separate things. They weren't, though. It was all part of the same problem. I wondered again about the fact that she kept using our bathroom. Perhaps a part of her had been reaching out, hoping one of us would notice.

I took a breath. "You should tell someone. Get some help."

That was it. Telling her she needed help was all I could do for her. The rest was up to her, and I didn't need to carry any responsibility for it anymore.

Clare stared at me, her expression a mix of confusion and something else I couldn't quite define. Then her face went hard.

"That's a bit rich coming from you, isn't it, Bailey?"

I didn't say anything. She stepped forward, getting right in my face, but I didn't move away. "Adam is the only person who can help me, and you took him away." Strings of saliva stretched between her lips. She wasn't crying, but she wasn't far from it.

"I didn't take Adam away from you, Clare," I said. I made my voice stay steady, though I felt anything but. For a moment I thought she was going to hit me, then she turned and walked out onto the deck. I followed her.

"I mean it. Get some help, Clare." I started shaking once the words were out of my mouth.

Clare stopped, but she didn't turn around.

"You're a horrible person." I'd never been so blunt to someone in my life, but now I'd started I couldn't stop. "You can't treat people like this. If you don't sort yourself out, you're going to be alone forever."

I heard the door behind me open, and Amber and Jenny came out of their room. I felt them hovering behind me, then Amber stepped forward, linking her arm through mine.

Clare stayed frozen, her heel raised in mid-step. For a moment, I thought she might turn back and face the chaos she'd created. Then she walked away without looking back.

My knees felt weak. I sat down on the deck and laid my head in my hands.

• • • •

JENNY CAUGHT UP WITH me as I was walking up to Gran's. She held out my earring. "Adam found this," she said.

I took it. There was dirt stuck between some of the beads, but it wasn't broken.

"He spent ages looking for it, the night of the dance." Jenny grinned. "But then he chickened out of actually giving it to you."

I stared at the earring. "Thank you," I said. I waited for Jenny to pipe up, telling me I should be thanking Adam, not her, but she held her tongue. I looked up. "And say thank you to Adam, too. Please," I added.

She gave me a hug. "I'm going to miss you! Amber will too. She wanted to say bye herself, but ..." Jenny chewed on her lip. "She's gone up to her parents' cabin." She made a face that was somewhere between a smile and a frown. "She said she was going to tell them the next time she talked to them." Jenny shrugged. "I don't know if she will."

I wasn't sure if there was anything I could say to that. Maybe Amber finally would face up to it, and talk to her parents. Maybe they would be fine with it. Or maybe she would chicken out and let the secret eat her for a little longer.

"I'd better get going," I said. "Tell Amber I said bye, though."

Jenny gave me another hug. "And you call me, once school starts back, okay?"

I nodded, though I knew I wouldn't.

Jenny rolled her eyes. "I've got your address, so if you *don't* call me I'll turn up on your doorstep!"

"I'll do my best," I said.

. . . .

WE GOT IN THE CAR AND drove away. Tilly was asleep in the back seat, and Gran was silent beside me. I couldn't tell what she was thinking, whether she was mad at me for not taking better care of Tilly, or whether she was just over the whole thing.

She was pulling out of the driveway, when I spotted Adam following us.

"Wait!"

Gran stopped the car, leaving it idling. I undid my seatbelt but didn't get out.

"Go on." Gran glanced over at me.

I walked over to Adam. He stood with his hands in his pockets, looking like he felt all the shame that Clare didn't.

"Thank you," I said.

He glanced up at me, squinting as the sun hit his face.

"For the earring. It was my mother's, and ..." I stared over his shoulder, back towards the resort. None of this was what I really needed to say. I looked back at him. "It was important," I said finally.

He nodded, then scuffed at the ground with his shoe.

I wondered if this was going to be it. The last time we ever talked, and it would be about nothing. Not even a conversation really, as he hadn't opened his mouth.

"I'm not coming back here." He looked up at me and gave a mouth shrug. "Mum and Jack probably still will, but ..." He shook his head. "I don't want to do this again."

I nodded. I think it was a big deal to him, to say he wasn't coming back. To actually say it out loud, I mean. A declaration of severed ties.

"Me neither," I said. "But I guess that's obvious."

He gave a half smile, and nodded. "I'd think you were crazy if you did."

I tilted my head in the direction of Gran's car. "Well, I'd better go."

"Yeah." He sighed the word, making it sound tired.

I turned away.

"You'll be in touch with Jenny, right?"

I looked back and nodded. He frowned and stared off into the distance. Finally he glanced back at me. "She has my number, so ..."

I hesitated. He could just give me his number himself, but that would come with an obligation. One he probably knew I wouldn't meet. "Okay," I said.

Adam bobbed his head and turned away, cutting through the paddock at the boundary of the resort grounds.

I walked back to the car and got back into the passenger seat. Gran glanced at me, but didn't ask. She started up the car and drove off.

Fifteen

I NEVER KNEW WHICH beach Mum and Dad met at. It probably wasn't in Paihia. Gran didn't move there until after she retired, so it wasn't Mum's home town. Going to the beach there felt like coming home, though. Getting in the water even more so.

"Do you want some more shells, Tilly?" Jenny asked.

Tilly didn't look up at her, just kept smoothing the sand out over the top of her castle. Jenny glanced at me and shrugged. True to her promise, she'd turned up on Gran's doorstep a couple of weeks after we got back. We'd gone to the beach together every Saturday since, often taking Tilly with us.

"You like the pink ones, don't you Till?" I asked.

Tilly still didn't look up, but she nodded slowly.

"Okay, we'll just get the pink ones then." I stood, then reached down to help Jenny up. I walked backwards so I could keep watching Tilly.

"Do you think she'll ever talk to me?" Jenny asked.

I shook my head. "She doesn't really talk to anyone much. Except me and Gran." I glanced up the beach to where Gran was sitting on a bench. She was wearing a long purple and blue silk scarf, making her easy to spot. It flowed around her shoulders like her own personal wave. There was no way she'd get in the actual water, though; it wasn't her style. In fact, I wouldn't have been surprised if she'd hidden a hip flask of gin and tonic in her handbag, just to pass the time.

Tilly looked up, and her face was panicked. I stopped, then took a couple of steps back towards her. She saw me, then started patting her castle again.

"That's further than you got last time," Jenny said.

I smiled. "Yeah. She's doing better for sure." I'd almost made it to the water this time. Tilly's counsellor had said she was opening up a little more. Only if I was in the waiting room, though. I wondered if she was ever going to be able to survive without me or Gran more than a few metres away.

Jenny sat down in the sand and started searching for shells. I stayed standing, making sure Tilly would be able to see me if she looked up again.

"Did you talk to Amber last night?" I asked. I knew the answer. They skyped every Friday night without fail. I knew Jenny would want to tell me about it, though.

Jenny swished her hand across the sand, disturbing only the first layer. She shook her head. "Bailey ..."

"What? Don't tell me her internet was down, again." I laughed, though that wasn't really funny.

Jenny didn't look up at me. She rolled a shell between her fingers, cleaning sand out from inside it. The sand collected under her nails instead, and she set the shell down to flick it out.

I frowned and crouched down beside her. "Hey, what's wrong? You guys didn't–"

"No, no we're fine." Jenny waved her hand, dismissing the idea that she and Amber could be having problems like it was ridiculous. "It's nothing like that. It's just ..." Jenny screwed up her face and continued in a rush. "I know you don't like surprises, and–"

I glanced back towards Tilly as Jenny hesitated. "Oh crap." I dashed back up the beach as a kid made a beeline for Tilly's sand castle.

Tilly looked up, but she didn't scream like she normally would. I slowed as I got closer. Jenny raced up the beach behind me.

"Jack," I said. I glanced back at Jenny.

She grinned, nervously. "Surprise."

I frowned. "But–"

"Hey, there you are!"

I looked up as Amber and Adam came down the dunes.

"We've been looking everywhere!" Amber raced down to meet Jenny, but Adam hung back.

He was wearing the same red board shorts he'd had on that first day at Pine Hills. It felt like a lifetime ago, when we'd frowned at each other across the pool. The board shorts seemed faded now. Less like blood, and more just red.

I sat down next to Tilly, looping my arm around her shoulder. She didn't look up at any of the new arrivals, but she kept patting her sand castle even when Jack joined her.

"Jack's come to see you, Tilly," I said.

She nodded, and for a moment I thought we were going to get a smile out of her.

"There was no way he was going to let me come alone." Adam came forward, hovering just near us.

I looked up at him, then nodded towards Amber. "I don't think there was ever a chance of that."

Amber and Jenny were bouncing, catching up on everything that had happened since they'd talked last night, I presumed. Amber's hair had grown out a bit, creeping down around her face in soft curls. It suited her. Pixie rather than ki-wifruit.

Adam flicked some sand towards me with his foot. I brushed it from my leg. I didn't know if he'd meant to do that, or if he'd just forgotten the sand was much more mobile than regular ground.

He squinted as the sun caught his eyes. "Can we go for a walk, Bailey?"

I glanced down at Tilly and frowned. "We can't go far."

Adam nodded and smiled. "I know. Jenny told me the drill."

I got up and retraced my backwards steps, this time with Adam beside me instead of Jenny. He walked slowly, swinging each step, to keep pace with me.

"So, you do this every week?"

I nodded. "Most weeks. It's working, though. The first time she came with us she wouldn't even let go of my hand." I stooped to pick up a shell, then kept walking.

Adam turned around, taking backward steps to match mine.

I shook my head. "It's okay. You don't have to walk back-wards."

He shrugged. "Change of pace." He glanced at me and grinned. "Literally."

I rolled my eyes at the joke. Jenny had made it on the first day too. I couldn't help a little smile creeping out.

Tilly hadn't looked up yet. Jack was talking to her. I don't think she was answering, but she seemed to be listening to him.

Adam's arm brushed mine. "Is it okay? That we came, I mean?"

I nodded. "Yeah. Tilly's doing better now, so she doesn't freak out with new people so much." Then I realised that probably wasn't what he meant. He was asking whether it was okay with me, not Tilly, since we hadn't exactly parted on the best terms.

"It's good to see you guys," I added. I nodded over to where Jenny and Amber were walking up the beach hand in hand. "Jenny's been missing Amber like crazy."

He rolled his eyes. "I know. I hear about it every shift."

"Shift?"

He grinned. "I quit McDonald's. I'm working–"

"At the pet store with Amber," I guessed, nodding my approval. "Much more vege-friendly."

"Jenny didn't tell you that?"

I shook my head. Jenny hadn't mentioned Adam to me at all. I knew she was in contact with him, and that he lived near Amber, but it had kind of been an unspoken agreement between us that we steered away from any conversation related to Pine Hills. She did tell me that Clare's parents had sent her to boarding school, when they found out about everything that had been going on. But when I told Jenny I didn't want to know, she didn't try again.

Adam sighed. "Jenny didn't even tell you we were coming, did she?"

I shook my head. "Not until about thirty seconds before you arrived." I laughed as he groaned. "It's okay, though. I'm better at surprises these days."

I glanced down as my feet hit the wet sand. A few more steps and I'd be in the water. I looked back at Tilly. She was actually looking up at Jack, meeting his eye.

I shook my head. "Amazing."

Adam paused beside me as I stopped walking. I felt, without turning to look at him, that he was watching Jack and Tilly too.

"You seem different," he said.

I wasn't sure if he meant it as a good or a bad thing, so I didn't answer. Of course I was different. Too much had happened for me not to be. I brushed the sand from my skin, not even flinching this time as my hand ran over the scar on my stomach. It had been like a dare, the first time I came to the beach in my bikini rather than covering up and hiding. Now I didn't even think about it.

He swallowed. "Jenny told me they finally found the guys who did it." He didn't clarify what he meant by that, but I knew.

I took a breath. "Yeah." I didn't say any more than that, and I hoped Adam wouldn't ask. As much as he had been right about it not bringing Mum and Dad back, it had made a difference knowing the police had found them. To me, if not to my parents. It still didn't make it easy to talk about, though. We would have to when it came time for the trial – the police said it was unavoidable. But they'd promised to make it as quick and simple as possible, and Tilly's counsellor would be there the whole time. Mine too.

"You bring your board?" I asked Adam.

He glanced at me. "Of course. You want a lesson?"

I nodded. "Gran's going to take Tilly home soon."

"I promised Jack a lesson, so maybe after that?"

"That'd be good."

I wondered if I could keep walking, just a little further, without Tilly freaking out. A few more steps and I'd feel the water rushing over my feet. A few more steps after that, and I could dive under the surface and disappear.

I glanced at Adam. "I think we should be friends," I said. I blushed as I heard how weird that sounded. I'd been going to say, "I think we should *just* be friends," but then I thought it might be presumptuous to indicate I'd ever thought there might have been something more. I hoped Adam would know what I meant, though, and would understand.

"Yeah?" He smiled his confusion.

I nodded. "Yeah."

He stared at me, his face flitting through a range of expressions again. I wondered if he'd felt it too, the awkwardness every time the two of us got close. Or if it had felt fine to him. I hoped he'd felt it too, and realised how much better it felt when we were just hanging out without the pressure of something more.

Adam smiled, and seemed to relax. "Okay."

It came back, then, that moment of calm I'd felt the first time I saw Adam sitting on the side of the pool. He looped his arm around my shoulder, pulling me into a sideways hug, and suddenly it wasn't awkward to be close to him anymore. Just nice.

I pulled away before I confused myself, and headed back up the beach even though Tilly hadn't looked up yet. "How's the sand castle going, Tilly?" I asked.

"Jack made a moat," she said.

"Did he? That's pretty cool."

"You got a bucket, Tilly?" Adam asked. "We should fill the moat with water."

Tilly didn't look at Adam.

I remembered the way Jack had stared at me if I spoke to him when Tilly wasn't there, and I wondered if Tilly too was simply shy at having a nearly-adult talk to her. Her fingers curled around the lip of the bucket beside her, though, and she pushed it towards Adam.

Adam grinned. "Come on, Jack. Let's go fill it up."

I sat down beside Tilly as they ran down to the water. "You okay, bub?"

Tilly nodded. "I like Jack."

Sometimes I felt like I was going to burst with how cute she was. I gave her a hug, but she squirmed away from me.

"Don't get me wet!" she squealed.

"I haven't even been in the water, you silly chicken." I laughed.

Adam and Jack ran back up the beach with the bucket of water, and Jenny and Amber came over as they poured it into the moat.

"Make a wish before the water sinks in!" Jenny yelled.

I laughed. "What?"

"Just do it!" She grabbed Amber's hand and squeezed her eyes tight shut. Amber looked at me and shrugged, but she closed her eyes too.

The water held for a moment, then sunk into the sand. I closed my eyes as the last few drops disappeared. There was a pause where we were all silent, then Jenny and Amber started laughing.

"You're so weird, Jenny!" Amber said.

I opened my eyes. The moat was dry again now, but the sand was still damp where the water had left its mark.

"Come on, let's go for a swim. You coming, Bailey?"

I shook my head at Amber. "You guys go ahead."

Jack was talking to Tilly, describing some plan for how to make the water stay for longer. I settled myself back on the sand. It was too cloudy to sunbathe, but that didn't stop me trying.

Adam sat down beside me. "What did you wish for?" he asked.

I glanced at him. "Not supposed to tell you that." I had actually made a wish this time, but I didn't want to say it out loud.

Adam shook his head. "It was wishing on water disappearing into sand. I don't think there are any rules."

I hesitated. I could claim superstition, and say I didn't want to tell him in case it didn't come true. I was wearing Mum's peacock feather earrings again, though, so I think it was obvious I'd left her superstitious influence well and truly behind. He probably wouldn't understand it, if I told him, so what did it matter anyway?

"I wished for today," I said finally. I lay my head back on my hand and stared at the sky.

Adam frowned like he thought he'd misheard me, then he nodded. It would be too hard to explain to anyone else, how you could wish for something that was already happening. It wasn't the same as wishing for things not to change, because I'd given up on the idea of that being possible. If anyone was going to get it, though, I thought Adam might.

He lay back on the sand next to me. "I wish for today too," he said. He reached out his hand, his little finger resting against mine. I didn't move for a moment, but I didn't let myself pull away either. Then I linked my fingers through his, squeezing his hand, and I could tell that made him smile.

I could have pointed out that the water was already gone, but I didn't. He was right. There weren't any rules. Even if there were, there was a whole ocean right in front of us, and a beach full of dry sand just waiting for the water to sink in.

Enjoyed this book? You can make a big difference.

Reviews are the most powerful tool when it comes to getting attention for my books.

As an indie author, it can be hard to get my books into the hands of readers, but honest reviews of my books help me do just that.

If you've enjoyed this book, I would be very grateful if you could spend just a few minutes leaving a review (it can be as short as you like).

Thank you very much!

BROKEN SILENCE

A stranger just put Kelsey's boyfriend in a coma. The worst part? She asked him to do it.

Seventeen-year-old Kelsey is dealing with a lot – an abusive boyfriend, a gravely ill mother, an absent father, and a confusing new love interest. After her boyfriend attacks her in public, a stranger on the end of the phone line offers to help. Kelsey pays little attention to his words, but the caller is deadly serious. Suddenly the people Kelsey loves are in danger, and only Kelsey knows it. Will Kelsey discover the identity of the caller before it's too late?

Broken Silence is the first young adult thriller from award-winning playwright Helen Vivienne Fletcher. If you like raw emotion, life-and-death suspense, and thrilling plot twists, then you'll love Helen Vivienne Fletcher's new page-turner.

Pick up *Broken Silence* now to discover the identity of Kelsey's Caller.

• • • •

SYMBOLIC DEATH

A woman finds a Death Curse symbol scratched into the soap scum around her sink.

A young boy watches his family fall apart after the death of his father.

A butterfly chrysalis hatches under the watchful eye of a hungry cat, and a teenage grim reaper's job is made harder by the boy who can see her.

Symbolic Death is a collection of sad, poignant, and darkly funny tales about death. If you like unique points of view, heart-breaking moments, and a touch of black humour, then you'll love Helen's short story collection.

Buy the ebook or paperback now or get it for free by joining Helen's mailing list at www.helenvfletcher.com.

Acknowledgements

A HUGE THANK YOU goes to the Wellington Children's Book Association, and to New Pacific Studios. I never thought I could write a book in a week, but having the time and space during the residency allowed me to do just that. I will be forever thankful to all involved for giving me the opportunity.

Another big thank you to all my friends and family for supporting my writing and publishing journey over the last year and a half. I know my brainstorming out loud must drive you nuts sometimes, but I love you all for nodding and smiling through it.

Finally, thank you to my wonderful same-name bestie, Helen, for beta reading, and to my amazing editor Sue Copsey, for all your help and encouragement.

About the Author

Helen Vivienne Fletcher has worked in many jobs, doing everything from theatre stage management to phone counselling. She discovered her passion for writing for young people while working as a youth support worker, and now helps children find their own passion for storytelling through her creative writing business, Brain Bunny Workshops.

Helen is the author of three picture books for children, and one short story collection. *Underwater* is her second young adult novel. She has won and been shortlisted for several writing competitions, including making the shortlist for the 2008 Joy Cowley Award, and in 2015 she was named outstanding new playwright at the Wellington Theatre Awards. Helen's poetry and short stories have appeared in various online and print publications, and she regularly performs her spoken word pieces around Wellington. Overall, Helen just loves telling stories, and is always excited when people want to hear or read them.

You can find Helen at www.helenvfletcher.com or connect with her on Facebook.

Read more at https://www.helenvfletcher.com/.